Praise for Jeannette Haien's *The All of It*

"The only book I know in which innocence follows experience. A truly amazing thing."

—Mark Strand

"What a beautiful little novel—perfection itself... A distinct and glorious triumph."

—Guy Davenport

"*The All of It*... is what a fellow reviewer friend of mine calls 'a good read,' and another friend would call 'a find.' Lovers of literary jargon might dub it a 'gem,' or a 'minor masterpiece.' It is all of these cliches and more.... You cannot help being impressed by this almost mythic story of secret lives and illicit loves."

—Doris Grumbach, National Public Radio

"Beautiful in its simplicity and directness, a gem of a novel."

—Amanda Heller, *Boston Globe*

"The story it tells makes one's breath quicken. What an extraordinary novel! I wouldn't say there are many novels of moral passion around.... But when one reads one, one remembers what a real novel can be."

—Paula Fox

"... the imaginative leap into lives of great simplicity and harshness is triumphantly achieved."

—*Financial Times*

"Jeannette Haien's first novel possesses the clear tone and the unpretentious manner which only the best writing achieves.... It cannot be too highly recommended."

—*The Literary Review*

The All of It

BY

Jeannette Haien

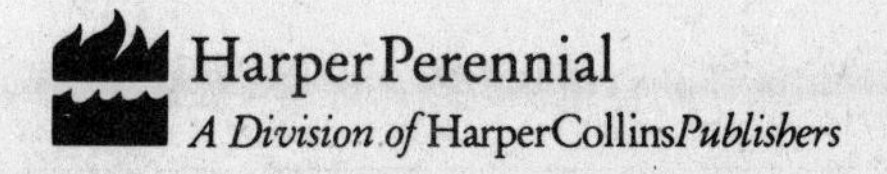

HarperPerennial
A Division of HarperCollins*Publishers*

A hardcover edition of this book was published in 1986 by David Godine, Publisher, Inc. It is here reprinted by arrangement with David Godine, Publisher, Inc.

First PERENNIAL LIBRARY edition published 1988.

Library of Congress Cataloging-in-Publication Data

Haien, Jeannette.
The all of it.

I. Title.
PS3558.A3255A78 1988 813'.54 87-45623
ISBN 0-06-097147-9 (pbk.)

---

96 RRD (H) 20 19 18 17 16

For Ernest Ballard

Author's Note

IN Ireland, stretches of a salmon-river which run through privately owned land are divided by the owner into sections, called "beats." Beats are let (rented) by the owner, by the day, to an angler. The angler is called the "rod." A "ghillie" (or "gillie") is a servant who attends the rod.

A "yirrol" is a year-old ewe.

The All of It

One

THOMAS DUNN, THE head ghillie at the Castle, wasn't telling Father Declan anything he didn't already know: the river too high and wild from all the rains, and the salmon, therefore, not moving, just lying on the bottom, not showing themselves at all, and the midges terrible, and only the two days left to the season so of course all but the least desirable of the river-beats, number Four, was let already; "and Frank and Peter'll be ghillieing for the Americans stayin' at the Castle, Father, so I'll have to give you Seamus O'Conner and he's hardly worth the pay and that on top of the twenty pounds for the beat and you know yourself, Father, how beat Four is after a rainfall such as we've been having, the piers awash and the banks slippery as grease. If you'd given me a bit more notice, if I'd but known you had it in your mind to come for the day, I'd have—"

The long-distance connection was weak; that, and Thomas's nattering on and on, discouraging, all but took the last of Father Declan's heart. Still, he'd do it. "I know all you're telling me, Thomas," he bawled into the mouthpiece of the parish-house phone, "I know. But I'll take beat Four and Seamus O'Conner with it, though I don't need him."

"It's the rule, Father, the hard and fast rule—a ghillie for every rod—not up to me, you know, but the Castle's."

"I know. So I'll be there at ten sharp in the morning, Thomas."

"If I'd but known, Father," Thomas began again, then started his coughing. "There's not a fish moving—"

"At ten then in the morning, Thomas."

"They're not moving, Father, I'm telling you. The water's too dirty and deep, they're just lyin' on the bottom, it'll not be worth it to you, the trip, gas and all, and no hope of a kill—"

"I'll not blame you, Thomas."

"So you'll be here tomorrow then, Father?"

"Yes, Thomas."

"It'll be good to see you, but I wouldn't want you to have your hopes up—"

"Don't worry about my hopes, Thomas."

"But as the day goes on, Father, if you change your mind about coming, just ring me back. I won't hold you to the cost of the beat."

"Thomas, listen: I'll not change my mind, and I've a funeral Mass at eleven. That's an hour from now, if you've your watch on, so I can't go on talking now."

"Of course, Father."

"So goodbye, Thomas."

Two

"IF 'TWERE ME, Father, given the conditions and all, I'd start off with a Hairy Mary, not that Stoat's Tail you're tyin' on."

Father Declan—Father Declan de Loughry in full—didn't honour the boy with a look, only the words, "But you're not me, Seamus O'Conner, are you now. And you're how old?"

"Eighteen last May."

"And I started fishing for salmon when I was eleven. That makes it fifty-two years now I've been deciding which lure to use. If you put those two figures together you'll have my age, the point being that I know what I'm doing."

Seamus—he cared not for experience—received

the information with a shrug. He lit another cigarette, his fourth since they'd left the Castle and arrived at the beat. Father Declan restrained himself from commenting on the number of his smokes; he knew Seamus would tell him he lit up against the midges, thick already, swarming in clouds from out of the wet foliage.

Right on cue, Seamus said, "Thomas warned me about the midges. Devils they are!"

Father Declan seized his chance: "They've put ridges on your neck already. . . . And that ear, boy! It's bleeding. . . ." Then, in his kindest tone: "You'd best go sit in the hut, Seamus, out of the way of them. . . . No, really now—I'll not hear otherwise. I'll call if I need you with the net."

But the boy protested: "Thomas said I'm to stay beside you."

"I'll account to Thomas if need be. You do as I say now." The words, spoken in a definite way, impressed Seamus as being final, and he sloped off, crashing in his gumboots through the furze and heather, his head bent down against the rain.

The stone hut, fond refuge of generations of anglers and their ghillies, was around the bend in the river, away, out of sight, and out of sight—gone—was exactly all that Father Declan wanted of Seamus O'Conner right at that moment.

He looked at his watch. 10:34. He positioned

himself and shook his rod several times to satisfy himself that its fittings were secure, after which, in the fullness of an angler's desiring, he made his first cast of the day.

Three

AFTER TWENTY-FIVE casts and strip-ins and not a sign of a rise (the river might as well be empty of fish, he thought, which it wasn't, of course, he knew) he changed the Stoat's Tail for a Silver Doctor. If Seamus hadn't suggested the Hairy Mary, he'd probably have gone to it next, but he couldn't do Seamus that favor: were a salmon to take the Hairy Mary, Seamus would glory, and it would be a false glory and bad for him as he had but small knowledge of the intricacies of the sport, his contact with it being that of an observer only (of meagre vigilance, Father Declan judged), and as listener to mouthings about it (after the fact of a kill) by toffs at the Castle bar; but no instinct for it, no sense of its mysteries or feel for the way, in your spine, you canny to where a salmon is lying, patient, in the river's dark undercurrents, and how your human patience connects to the creature's patience, the determination in yourself and the steel of your concentration alike to the fish's wait and wiliness. *That*, Seamus knew naught of, nor could it ever be explained to him. . . .

Four

"EXPLAIN, KEVIN, explain! Confess!"

Only four days ago, Kevin, ill unto death, had revealed to Father Declan that he and Enda, his supposed wife of many years, were, in fact, not married.

Appalled, and in a torment for Kevin's soul, Father Declan urged upon Kevin that he marry Enda at once. Kevin, though, only waved a weak hand through the air: "It can't be done, Father. There's a reason—"

"What *reason*, man? Explain, Kevin! Confess!"

"Ah, Father, you've said it yourself from the pulpit, that there's some explanations as get you nowhere."

"Try! You must. *Hear* me, Kevin."

But all the strife and urgency was Father Declan's. Kevin said, "Not now," and looked away; then back. "There's a day or two left in me still, Father. There's time, I mean to say. . . . The wind—it's risen, has it?" and to Father Declan's nod: "Would you be so kind as to bring Enda in now? She'll take a chill outdoors in the weather."

"I will."

He walked through the raw of the clouded afternoon to the back of the house. "Enda?" he called softly.

She answered from just inside the door of the cattle-fold, "Here, Father," showing herself, shawled; and as he approached: "Kevin, he told you, Father? About us?"—her eyes immense.

"He did. . . . And you, Enda, you'd best lose no time confessing!" His eyebrows came together. "I'm personally mortified for the two of you. What have you been thinking of all these many years"—Enda's eyes strayed over the yard— "before God with your sin," he went on sternly, "and deceiving your neighbors—"

"The question never came up," she cut in.

"Because you saw to it that it didn't, did you not, you and Kevin, pretending so well at being Mr. and Mrs. And myself, serving this parish for the past five years, thinking I had your trust, and not a word. Nor Father Francis before me nor the priest before him. *Shame*, Enda," he growled, and as she still said nothing, only stood straighter, he plied her fiercely with: "And why will Kevin not marry you now?" leaning a little towards her.

"Ah, you went into that with him, did you?" Her eyes narrowed.

"Of course," he answered sternly, " 'Tis my duty."

"I understand, Father." Her manner, careful until now, gentled. She made a gesture of appeal. "You mustn't take it so hard, Father," she went on softly; "There's a part you don't know—"

"So Kevin said," he interrupted darkly.

"I gave him my word I'd not be the first to speak of it." She hesitated; then: "Do you feel, Father, as you've seen him today, that his time's coming on fast now?"

"I do." He opened out his hands to her: "Tell him, Enda, to confess fully when next I come. There's no sin past God's forgiveness."

She nodded vaguely. He thought she was going to say something more, but she didn't—only brushed his sleeve with her hand, then walked quickly from him into the house.

Five

THE NEXT DAY, sinking fast—he would die but a few minutes later—Kevin said weakly, "It's for me to tell you, Father." He lay in a narrow rut of mattress on the extreme right side of the double bed. Enda had again absented herself to the cattle-fold. Father Declan, from his close-drawn chair, reached out and touched the dying man's arm. "For me to tell," Kevin repeated. " 'Tis a harsh thing, Father."

"It's my purpose to hear it, Kevin, and for God in His mercy to judge and forgive."

A low and awful rasp came from Kevin's throat; a sudden moisture caused his forehead to gleam. His eyes made a frantic sweep of the room.

"Here, man. . . . Steady. I'm here, Kevin."

"Aye, Father."

Twice, in gulps, Kevin swallowed. "Enda," he began, "my fear's for Enda, Father, that you'll rage against her, being human as you are." Again, the frantic look away.

"Kevin, you *know*, surely you must: I'd not ever go against Enda."

"Human you are, like the rest of us, despite the collar, forgive me, Father—" Again, from his throat, the low, dark churr; then a spasm that crazied his body and lit his eyes in subjugation.

Father Declan asked: "Do you want Enda?"

But Kevin shook his head and, thick-tongued, whispered, "I'll tell thee, but swear to me first" —with a brilliant last strength—"swear to me, Father, you'll stand by Enda. *Swear it.*"

"I swear, Kevin. And I say again to you, it's not for me to judge, but for God, and for Him to understand and forgive."

"*God!*" Kevin uttered passionately. With a frenzied movement he appeared to try to lift himself up towards the word that had burst so violently from his lips. Briefly, his hands did battle with the air, then dropped like shot birds, smallened and still, onto his heaving torso. He opened his mouth, but no words came. The seizure had silenced him forever.

Through the thunder of the ensuing silence, Father Declan spoke his name: "Kevin. . . . Kevin. . . ."

Kevin heard and nodded. But his face had gone lax, and his eyes, nested in resignation, were lustreless.

Father Declan knew the sign: that suspension of physical and spiritual pain which is given to some just prior to death. He put his lips to Kevin's forehead and spoke gently into his ear: "I'll get Enda."

He walked to the door of the house, which stood open to the noon's light. Outside, he hurried to the back yard. From the cattle-fold, Enda saw him and came running to his side. "He's not gone?" she whispered imperatively.

He sought her eyes: "No, but you'd best be with us now, Enda dear."

She plucked at his sleeve: "Did he tell you of us?"

"He tried. He meant to. But he had a seizure." Then, with a gesture of helplessness, "You should know, Enda—the seizure—he can't speak."

"Ah," she breathed, looking off.

"Come," he told her.

Inside, she approached the bed and knelt by its side. Her eyes rested deeply on Kevin's face but—it was as if some agreement had been reached between them—she made no move with her hand towards his fixed open one.

Summoning all his strength, Father Declan commenced the sacrament of extreme unction.

Six

Enda had pled, "You'll see to it, Father? have the death notice printed just as I've said it to you, just as Catherine McPhillemy had it done when Sorley died?"

Father Declan's eyes met the black of her own. After a low, white cry of grief—Kevin lay but minutes dead on the bed—she had begun a murmurous weeping alike to the run of the hillside rivulet outside the house. Moments later the weeping ceased and gave way to the appeal she put to him with a compellingly odd urgency: "You'll see to it, Father? Have the death notice printed—you will, Father?"

"You ask too much of me, Enda," he'd protested, "wanting me to see to the printing of a lie. 'Tis a furtherance of the sin." The charge—it was his duty to make it—caused in him, by the responding lance of Enda's eyes going suddenly darker and condemned, a rush of pity, and he said kindly, in a reasoning way, "It'll be another thing you'll have to account for, another guilt you'll have to bear. . . . A public notice of that sort—it should be the truth, Enda," he shifted his feet, faltering before her tears. "And as we both know yourself and Kevin weren't married," he warmed to the subject now, "and as the two of you wouldn't hear of letting me marry you before Kevin died—"

"Kevin told you, there's a reason," she interrupted.

"And died, he did, God rest his soul, before he could give me the reason," he replied, "so I'm further in the dark," fixing her in his gaze.

"So it's for me to tell you now, Father," she answered urgently.

"Not now, Enda. And not here. In the confessional stall is where I'll hear it."

She shot him a warrior's look: "If I give you my word, Father, that our reason, Kevin's and mine, for not marrying—that you'll understand it once I make it known to you and that it'll not add to the lie, but *explain* it—will you not, I beg you, have the notice printed? There'll be, you see, no peace for me ever again if you don't."

"Enda—"

"Please, Father," she whispered, "Please."

He turned his gaze to the dead man, then back to her. He told her, "God forgive me, I'll do it."

Her eyes softened. "And I'll do whatever penance is proper; whatever you lay on me, Father."

He said, "I've not been postured like this before."

"I appreciate that you've not, Father. But it'll come right for you when I tell you."

"So I'll go now," he told her. "I'll see to the undertaker. . . ." She helped him with his coat. "I'll be back to you no later than five o'clock. . . . You'll be all right, Enda?"

"Aye, Father."

Down the rutted lane he stopped at the first cottage—Catherine McPhillemy's—to tell Catherine Kevin had died at last. "I'll go straight to Enda," Catherine said. In Roonatellin, he stopped four times, giving out word of Kevin's death.

At the district newspaper office, to the fussy man with steel-rimmed glasses, he said, "Print it just as I've written it out if you will, please."

"Of course, Father. It's entirely legible."

He took out his wallet. Having entered into the sin of the lie, he would pay for the worldly end of it out of his own pocket.

Seven

DENNEHY *(Roonatellin, County Mayo) September 22,* 1982 *at the age of 63, Kevin, beloved husband of Enda; deeply regretted by his loving wife. R.I.P. Funeral on Friday (September 24) after 11:00 o'c Mass at St. Fintan's Cemetery.*

Eight

AT NOONTIME THE quiet rain that had persisted throughout the morning turned to a slanted, splattering downpour that beat against his face and seeped down into the collar of his green slicker, sogging his neck. Yet he persisted at his casting, sometimes almost blindly, the teem being that thick.

He kept thinking he shouldn't be there in the rain and cold, the midges eating him alive—worse than any telling of a hair-shirt—and the river swollen to boisterousness; shouldn't be there because there's no point to fishing if you can't concentrate. Yearning, he recalled the times in his life when he'd fished well through midge-ridden days in weather even meaner than this, and how, adroitly, Nature had put her claim on him and made him one with the very ground at his feet, and how, with every cast, past the gleaming green reeds of the shoreline shallows, he'd projected himself towards a specific spot in the river's very heart, a different shading in the water that was like a quality of seriousness, or at a laze in the current's glide, some *felt* allurement of expectation which became (ah, fated fish) the focused haven of his energy.

Hopeless, today: everywhere he looked he saw Enda's face; in every sound he heard Enda's voice: in all the world (or so he felt) there was only her and himself. . . .

At half-twelve Seamus came lumping through the rain. "You must be wanting your lunch, Father."

He managed a smile. "Not yet. But have yours, Seamus. I'll take a sandwich later. . . . And stick to the hut."

But the boy maddeningly lingered.

Some time ago, he'd given up on the Silver Doctor and replaced it with a Blue Charm. Now Seamus caught him in the act of discarding the Blue Charm for a Silver Rat. Under Seamus's eye, his hands, red and clumsy from the cold, shook.

"Thomas warned me 'twould be a useless day," Seamus vouched.

"Will you stop it, boy!" he cried. "Is there nothing in you but complaints? *Go*, I'm telling you, and permit me to get on with my fishing."

Seamus gave him one of those low, sidelong glances common to youths these days, then said, "Just as you will, Father," and walked away, bent, as he'd come, against the downpour.

Alone again, with the Silver Rat secured, he raised his rod and set to afresh: cast, strip, cast, strip, cast. . . . Once, he looked up and took in the density of the cloud-cover over the mountains, the peaks lost to view, and, from the southwest, a further, blacker pile-up of scud being winded in from the sea.

A terrible day.

And what would Enda be doing now, this first day after Kevin's funeral, this Saturday? If he had to name a time and a day of the week that called to mind Kevin and Enda as a pair, it would be mid-morning of a Saturday-shopping-day. That was when you'd see them, in all weather, sailing on their bicycles down the long hill into Roonatellin to do their week's marketing. They always rode right alongside each other like gleeful, strong children, their heads high and their faces lit in a transport of excitement as the wheels of their bikes rolled faster and faster. . . . Out in his old Ford, making his Saturday calls on the shut-ins, he'd often come upon them as they rode towards town; always, he would honk and wave, and one or both of them would give a swift, hand-reflex kind of a salute, but he never knew whether they took in who was greeting them, for their eyes never lifted from the thrilling coming-on thread of the road. The sun on them or rain, or a switch of wind whipping them—it didn't matter—they exuded some high, terribly intense, obliterating joy, which—it haunted him now—more than once had inflamed his imagination to raw conjecturings . . . suppressed to the greater marvelment that, to Enda's able arms, God had given no child to hold.

Would he ever get over the sadness of the truth of it?

Enda: when he'd returned to her after seeing to the publishing of the lie, running out, at the sound of his car, into the dusk-shadowed yard: "You're back, Father, thank God. And you went to the news-office?"

"I did. It'll be printed just as you wanted in the morning's paper."

"Come in, Father."

All had been done: Kevin laid out, washed and shaved, clothed in his black Sunday suit, his rosary twined between his fingers. At each corner of the bed a candle burned; the spaced glimmerings offered the only light in the room.

"Catherine helped me," Enda said simply.

They knelt at the foot of the bed and separately prayed.

When he stood again, Enda stirred but remained

at her kneel. "I'll tell you the all of it now, Father," she said, looking up at him.

He disowned a secular urge to reach down and lift her up. He told her instead, "Here, Enda"—turning a chair around for her—"sit here. . . ." And as she complied: "Now, Enda dear, understand me when I tell you you should better save for the confessional what it is you're wanting to tell me."

"No," she said.

"No?"

"No." She stiffened, hawk-like.

"And why not?" he challenged.

"It has not to do with God."

"Everything has to do with God," he replied firmly.

She shook her head, denying. "If you'll but hear it you'll see 'tis outside God." Then, flushing, her eyes hard on his: "I'll tell you now or never."

The threat (for so it struck him as being) made him cry out to her: "Enda!"—admonishing.

She flinched; her eyes went wide, but she held firm. "Now or never," she repeated.

In an effort to size her resolve, he regarded her deeply. She met his gaze levelly and fiercely. It was then of course he should have reminded her of the Church and of himself as an agent of God, and, unless she relented, refused her the hearing. But he saw she would not relent, her resolve being, he could tell, as iron. And . . . *there*, touchable for its closeness, was Kevin's body, shell of his life, reminding; but profounder was Enda herself, waiting out the long moment of his ruling silence with a dauntlessness that sworded him through with pity and fascination.

It was as he continued to study her that the persuasion came upon him that for all her seeming strength of will, she was in some way fearful. If such was the case, he told himself, he had no choice but to allow her her say.

Still, he felt he must state his misgivings. "It's against my better judgement to hear you as you oblige me to," he began solemnly, bringing his hands together, his eyes staying on her, "but as it means so much to you, I will, nevertheless."

"As you put it, Father, that is to say, if it means pressing it on you, it needn't be done," she answered proudly.

What could he but admire her? He made a gesture of measured conciliation, then: "I appreciate, Enda, that it'll be no easier for you to tell than for me to hear."

Her brow cleared. She said, "Thank you, Father." She stood up. "I've water boiling. I'll just give us some tea. . . . Take a chair for yourself." Still, though, she hesitated. "You'll need to be patient, Father," she qualified.

"I will of course, Enda."

"—not stop me over the first thing I tell you—"

"I won't."

"—hear me through to the end, I mean."

She turned from him towards the bed and stood for what seemed to him to be an immense length of time, her back to him as she looked at Kevin's face. In his chair, he waited, feeling large and uncollared. He shifted his feet. His shoes made a soft, scurring sound on the floor.

She shuddered.

As long as it would be granted him to live, he would remember how, then, her spine straightened as she filled her lungs with a diver's deep breath, and how, just before she plunged into the violent waters of her telling, she turned back to him, her eyes glistening and entreating and charged with courage, and, finally, how the sped words fell: "You have to know, Father—Kevin and myself, we're brother and sister."

Nine

AT HALF-ONE, HE rested his rod in the thorny tangle of a furze-clump and made his way to the ghillie hut.

Inside it, Seamus sat, his back braced against a post, his torso scrunched forward over his folded arms. "Giving up, Father?" he asked in an itching way.

He restrained himself: "No, Seamus. I've come for my lunch." Then, acidly: "I don't like to disturb you, boy, but if you could just manage to reach out and hand me the thermos, I could use some hot tea."

"There's not much left. It bein' so cold, I—"

"I'll take what there is, thank you, Seamus." It was a blessing just to sit down. From the strenuous efforts of casting, his shoulders ached, and his legs, too, from standing so long. Morosely, Seamus watched him as he ate his sandwich and drank a comforting cup of tea.

Of the two sheep grazing near the hut's open door Seamus remarked, "Them's lucky, havin' them heavy coats."

"I take it you're cold, Seamus. . . . You might try going outside and moving about."

"But for the rain—"

"Ah, the rain again, is it?" forcing a smile. "You're right of course, Seamus. I'm sopped through myself."

"You'll take a chill, Father," the boy argued. "You've given it a noble try, but Thomas is right, it's no good in this weather, the water's too high and the fish—"

"—just lie on the bottom, not moving," he finished the cant for him. "You'd advise me to give off, then?"

"I would, Father."

"Well now, Seamus, I'll tell you what I'm going to do. . . . I'm going to nap for a few minutes, and then I'm going back to my fishing. Now if you'll draw the door to against the wind—"

There's benefaction to closing off vision: with your eyes shut you're disobliged from keeping the show going for yourself or anyone else. . . . So thinking, he briefly dozed.

"Did I snore, Seamus?" coming awake a bit later.

"Aye," Seamus grinned.

"Well . . ." he stretched. "It's time I was leaving you again, Seamus." He stood up. "Keep the net handy." He had to say that.

It was raining still: fate of the day. And the midges swarmed, thicker than ever. Back on the beat, he saturated his face and neck and hands with a commercial bug-deterrent: but for its feeble effect, he'd be eaten alive. He'd try now, he decided, a Thunder and Lightning . . . and tied it on, feeling as he did so a hopelessness of purpose akin to anger. Then he positioned himself anew and in a kind of desperate, stubborn rage, he began again: cast, strip, cast, strip, cast. . . .

What clue had he missed, what giveaway indication of Kevin's and Enda's sibling relationship? No inkling from an examination of their conjured physical and characteristic selves: he had been through that earlier in the day, had, all the long miles of the drive over from Roonatellin to the Castle, imaged in his mind their faces and bodies and the way they thought and the way they moved, scrutinizing every detail. To no avail. Kevin: with his straight, light, soft hair (the merest breeze could randomly part it); his blue eyes that tended easily to water over; the mould of his features expressive more of determination than of intelligence; his nimble-jointed body (he could go up a ladder and come down it with a crazy ease that drew smiles);

his tendency in leisure to keep to a ready neatness, as if he were subject at all times to an imperative call; his easy laugh, but his empty silences; his broad, blunt, capable hands; his tedious care of tools; his impetuous though untheatrical generosity; his near-dull, incurious adherence to the palpable perimeter of his immediate, personal world: for him, the horizon held no allure.

A far, far different coin of spending was Enda, daughtered historically, he fancied, of the race of Heber, the eldest son of Milesius, King of Spain, who, as Dublin-bred, educated schoolboys of his generation had learnt, colonized Ireland early on, way, way back. Hers the abundant, curly, enticingly coarse raven-dark hair of that Iberian breed; hers the black, changing eyes gifted, in conjunct with a subtle intellect, to sightings of the intuitive sort; hers the elegant, long-fingered, obscurely imperious hands; hers a spontaneity of response, sexually illusory; hers a sailor's canniness (kindness came after); hers—Kevin's never—the lit, brilliant face set in the direction of, and becalmed in, distance.

That disalike they were, one from the other.

Two other elements mightily distinguished Enda from Kevin. Firstly: Enda could read—a bit (Kevin not at all)—and she had sought and acquired this skill, however limited, as an adult, by going and sitting over a period of months with the "beginning learners" at the state school in Roonatellin; and though her ease with the printed word was rudimentary—no more than that of a child—she regularly pored over and practiced her skill on the instrument of the district newspaper. Her progress, as one watched her at it, through the prose of that simple sheet, was slow-gaited and awesomely sombre, but, for the gist and feel of fact and life which she arduously gleaned from it, terribly satisfying to her.

Secondly: she possessed a naturally aristocratic and emotionally connective approach to the spoken word; she cared about how she said what she wanted to say. In the middle of a sentence she would often hesitate, and one knew she was searching for the better phrase or the more telling word. This concern particularized and lent to each of her relationships an intrinsic delicacy. Her verbal falterings had always fascinated him for the ways in which they revealed the workings of her mind and for the fact of their being infatuatingly expressive of herself.

Yet, of Kevin and Enda as a pair—shouldn't he have guessed *something*? But by what means? The habits of their lives had been so ordinary-seeming, their expectations so simple, Kevin tending to his small acreage and his sheep and taking on odd jobs for the extra, and Enda abiding so gladsomely over the home-hearth, the two of them showing every evidence of love of God, being regular and humble and joyful in their worship. Enda especially; Sunday after Sunday—Sundays were the day for Enda—she'd be on her knees at early Mass, the rosary in her hands and the world lost on her for all her raptness. Thrilling, the grace of her gathered self at prayer.

Still—and he perceived it in a rush—there *had* been something, a signal, if he'd but put it to use, whose possible significance he himself, within himself, had always sought to gainsay. For there: the fact of it, that in all the parish, no other pair of any age—displaying engaged twosomes or quick-talking new-marrieds or elderly couples bonded in long wedlock—none but Kevin and Enda gave off, as they were seen standing together or sitting next to each other, that stirring element, that *given*, like a scent of unalterable persuasion, of hardness. *Purpose*: that was the word which sprang consequentially to mind.

What he would never get over, as Enda told it to him that late afternoon after Kevin's death, was the sorrow of the usualness of her and Kevin's early childhood: their mother dying giving stillborn birth to her third child—that when Kevin was three and Enda two; and after their mother's death, their young, distraught, overburdened father going queerer and queerer, colder and colder, caring finally for nothing—not himself or his children or his land or livestock—finding in drink his only refuge.

"You've been up Donegal way, Father? So you know how it is there, the mountains like walls and the thick hills between one glen and the other and the land in the glens sweeping up and off as far as ever you can see, stretches of no one and nothing but clouds and rocks and sheep grazing and now and then a house set down in the reaches. Ours was such a one. Nowhere, it was. Just sheep-tracks making to it, and them wiped out often by the rains. . . .

"Of course, I'm talking fifty, sixty years ago. Now it's changed I suppose, Donegal being just as likely to change as anyplace else. There's cars now for one thing, and cars get everywhere, wanted or not. But at the time I'm talking of, when Kevin and myself were children, there'd be weeks and weeks when we'd not see a soul except for ourselves and our dad. . . . Oh, of course, we got to Mass when we could, though the church was a fast hour's walk from our house, that apart we were. . . ."

He knew the image: the widower appearing on the Lord's day with his haphazardly-clad children, the lot of them large-eyed and yearning and holding back like shy, uncertain creatures of the field. "You had no relatives, Enda? No aunts? No uncles? No relations of any sort? None at all?" he asked.

No one. Apparently there had been no one. Or perhaps—Enda's memory was vague—there had been someone she recalled as being mentioned, a great-aunt of her mother's, but there had been a rupture of the tie, a quarrel of some sort, so the great-aunt in reality was no more than a figure in a dream.

". . . but at the best, had there been anyone, they'd not likely have ventured the distance to our place to look in on us," Enda went on. Then, with a shrug: "These days of course, for a family in our fix, there's all the State Social Services and the county officials looking into every nook and cranny of your life, and as I said, cars. It's cars that's made the most difference. But we'd none of that I've just mentioned. For us, back then, it was like we weren't known as being alive."

She said that cutting sentence, then shocked him by laughing. ". . . Not that we thought that then, for we knew no other life, and you can't know what you don't know, isn't it so, Father? And we were busy, morning to night, Kevin at doing on the place—our dad put him early to doing a man's work, and me hauling and fetching, washing and mending and cooking, both of us doing a grownup's workaday. Only little we were—six and seven, no bigger than that." Again, her strange, marvelling laughter and her following, "Aye; and we did our work well, too. . . ."

She took a swallow of her tea. "The house in Donegal was of stone. Not grand, I don't mean to say, but not a mere place such as this, having as it did an upstairs with one room. That room—" she seemed for a moment confused, but recovered herself quickly enough and went on: "—all the time we were small our dad kept the room forever locked. We never saw him go near the stairs that led up to it, though when he'd sit at table we'd often see his eyes stray up the stairs. But his feet, never. Kevin and myself . . . we'd got it hard once for playing on the stairs and it fixed us against going near them again. . . . Well, except for myself. On Saturdays. Our dad would have me put a dust-cloth to the steps each Saturday. He was fierce about that regular dusting. I'd do the cloth over one step at a time, and then I'd be at the top, you know, right at the door to the room—him watching me—and the minute I finished up there, he'd point for me to come down."

"You never asked your dad about the room, Enda? You nor Kevin?" he asked gently.

She turned on him a face fired with frustration: "I can tell it's hopeless, Father."

"Hopeless?"

"Speaking of it. There's no way to get it across to you"—she spoke through her teeth—"the fear we had of our dad."

"Ah, I see. Forgive me, Enda. But I see now—"

"You *have* to see," she said deeply. "If you're to understand, you have to."

"I do. I see now. Believe me, Enda."

"So, I'll go on then?"

"Please, Enda."

"I can't say I didn't wonder about the room, but only to myself. I didn't, I mean, ever talk to Kevin about it. That I didn't had to do with the fear of our dad, like as if he'd *know* if myself and Kevin were to talk of it and get himself in a rage and take it out on us. Do you follow me, Father?" And at his nod: "One day, Kevin was twelve when this happened, and me eleven—and I don't know what brought it on—our dad went terrible queer, called Kevin and me to him and told us, 'We'll be clearing out that upstairs room now.' He had a big black key in his hand and he spent some time in showing it to us, holding it up close to our faces, all the time saying it was time now to clear out the room. He'd not been drinking but he was that queer-looking, very far off he seemed to be, but *there*, tall, right over us, but *not* at the same time. . . . I'm hard put to say how it was."

"I understand all you're saying, Enda."

"Yes. . . . Well, he started us up the stairs, rough, having us go before him. I snatched a look at Kevin. He was white as a sheet. I took hold of his sleeve, just to hang onto like, but our dad reached up and tore my hand off it, I don't to this day know why, except maybe as he decided to come between us. . . . When he put the key to the lock he said to us, 'It's all to be cleared out and all of it burned.' He had trouble with the lock and that got him frantic, but it let at last and he put us in through the door. . . ." She stopped.

"It's all right, Enda dear. Take your time."

"I've not talked of it before," she explained. "All these years, Kevin and myself never made mention of that day. . . . It's necessary I tell you of it, though, Father, you'll see why. . . ." and to his encouraging nod: "It turned out the room had been our dad's and our mother's. The minute we were in it we understood that, the way you do, you know, not that you're told, but that it comes clear to you. All our dad said was, 'It's to be emptied out,' and he started in, pulling at the bed, raving at us to give him a hand down the stairs with the mattress. . . . It wasn't a big job, the clearing-out, there being only the mattress and the wooden bed-frame and a chair. Oh, and a table, very small and rickety. Everything was filthy with mould from the damp. Green, you know. Mildew. And creatures had got to the mattress so the stuff was out of it in places and it smelled. . . ." She faltered, but only slightly. "There was one final thing in the room, a clothes-rack, thick with cobwebs and two dresses hanging from it—in tatters they were—and our dad . . . ," she raised her hand as if fending off a blow, ". . . our dad flew at the dresses like a rook on a dead rabbit, ripping and tearing at them, his eyes wild. The dresses . . ." she seemed unable to go on.

". . . were your mother's," he supplied for her.

She nodded quickly, and in the field of his resting gaze cast upon him a look that caused him to feel he was being greeted. "You do see," she said with a linking show of relief.

"I do. I do, Enda." He would have liked to touch her, to make some show of reassurance, but asked instead, wanting to help her along: "And *was* everything burned?"

She nodded again, still with her eyes in the clasp of his. "All of it," she said, "with Kevin and me looking on. He—our dad—had us to look on."

"And then?"

"Over the fire—it was a long time burning—our dad quieted down, drew in on himself you might say, and when the fire burned out, he told Kevin and myself that the next thing we were to do was to lock the room tight shut again and that after we'd done that we'd have done all that must be done. . . . What he meant was he would do the locking, and Kevin and me the watching of him at the doing of it. . . . He made a great thing out of locking the door, Father, put himself against it after the bolt took, and shoved at it and turned the knob over and over, making sure like, and when he was satisfied holding the key close up to our faces again before he put it in his pocket. And then—I don't know—with the key in his pocket, he seemed very pleased, had that look on his face of having struck a good bargain for his yirrols on fair-day. . . . And—that was the end of it, Father."

He let her have a full moment, appreciating her need of it. Then: "The end of it, Enda, as to your dad and the room, you mean?"

She reacted to the question almost frantically, like a slack labourer who, caught in a drowse, and roused, hectically reaches out for the nearest set-down tool: "To the end of clearing it out," she picked up, nodding violently. "But the room"—her eyes, in the candlelight, glittered with a sudden unnatural excitement—"the room came to figure for Kevin and me."

Her agitation drew his hand to her arm, laid there to calm and reassure, but barely offered, withdrawn, the gesture challenged by the greater force of her concentration.

"Our dad took to caging us up in it. . . . The first time—it was about six months after we'd cleared it out—he got very quiet and private-like the way he could, and he called us to him and took us up the stairs and put us in the room, telling us he'd let us out when the time was right. Those were his words—'When the time is right,' he said.

Then he left us, locking the door behind him. Kevin and myself, we were that upset as to not venture a whisper between us to pass the time, just sat, waiting on the bare floor like a pair of birds with the tongues cut out of them."

"How long?"

"The whole of the afternoon," she answered softly, then turned her eyes from him to the opposite wall and stared at it in so melancholy and mesmerized a way as to cause him to suppose she perceived its blankness as the inverse of every marking life had inflicted on herself.

"Enda, dear?"

She started. "Oh," she breathed, present again, bustling: "Your tea, Father. I'll just strengthen it."

"No, no. Don't get up."

She did get up, though, and poured out fresh cups for them, then fetched, from the corner stall, two sods of turf, adding them to the fire and stirring it. When she returned to her place, she seemed refreshed, like someone who has inhaled a stimulating draught of cold air. But as he looked closely at her, he saw he was misreading the look on her face, that it had nothing to do with stimulation, but was rather the sharp aspect of determination.

"Over the next couple of years, our dad would do that, lock us up every so often, whenever it came over him to do it. There was never a way of knowing when it would be, not until it happened, if you follow me. . . . There'd be just his calling of us to him and our knowing by the manner of him when we got to him what was in store for us. . . . He was drinking more and more. A terrible lot. He'd take off on the long hike to town, you know, of a morning, and come back at dusk-time and you wouldn't know how he could have made it home, how it was he didn't fall and break a bone, stumbling all the way and the ground so uneven, full of stones and ruts. . . . Drink brought out the temper in him, too. Kevin took the worst of that. You'd not believe the strappings Kevin stood up to, Father, and not a sound out of him." She brought her hands together: "I . . . I don't know . . . it was always different, but always the same, too, the locking-up of us, until the time I'm to tell you about. That was in February. . . . It was a terrible cold winter that year. . . . We'd had one snowfall after another and it'd stayed in the slope-hollows. There'd been no sun for days, just the snow and sleet and the nightly freeze and more snow, regular-like, over and over. . . . This time I'm telling you of, we'd got up in the morning—"

"How old were you?" he interrupted, having to know.

"Fifteen, Kevin was, and myself just turned fourteen. . . . As I was saying, we'd got up that morning and I was just pouring out the tea when our dad said to put down our cups and get up the stairs, he had things to do in town, he said, and no time to waste. He was wild-like, and he started in telling us how our mother always liked for us to be with her when he went into town and how now we had to get upstairs to her right away as she was tidying the room and he had to be off. Raving crazy he was, in a way we'd never heard from him before. That, his crazy-talking, and the queerness coming on him at the first of the day—well, we knew to mind him. It wouldn't have done to cross him, I mean." She stopped. "You're looking at me in such a way, Father. . . . You're following me all right?"

"Yes, Enda. Truly."

She cast upon him a speaking look, but remained silent.

He inclined himself towards her: "You've all my regard," he told her imperatively.

She nodded like a restless dreamer. "Well, he put us in the room, but before he locked the door on us, he stood a long time just looking around, turning his head this way and that, feverish-like, you know. Jacked-up. Then, it was like he'd settled on something in his mind, he turned around and went out, locking us in after him. He locked up the whole house that day, front and back. We heard him at it, sealing us in every way he could. Then he went off, yelling to us he'd be back after he'd seen to his affairs."

She broke off and looked towards the bed. He saw the swift tears come into her eyes. "Enda," he said, "spare yourself, Enda dear. . . . Leave off for now. Tomorrow—"

She drew a breath. "No," she whispered. "I'll finish with it. It's for me to finish with now . . . ," and, lifting her head: "The room had but a slit of a window in it. You know the kind—"

"I do," he said, knowing bitterly well the deep, set-in type still to be seen in houses built at the time the English levied the window-tax. "I do," he repeated. "Slits, as you say. Narrow as your fist."

"Aye. . . . That window and some breaks in the rotted-out roofing, that was all the light in the room. . . . I told you the house was of stone? Well, the room wasn't plastered but for the one wall the door was set in, and the stones—the stones had the winter cold stored up in them. . . . It happened all so fast, our dad putting us in the room and all, we'd not thought, Kevin nor me, to grab onto an extra bit of a jacket or a sweater. . . ." She faltered, made an empty gesture, then added, "We didn't know to." She swallowed. "I'll not draw it out, Father. We got through the day, long as it was, knowing as we did our dad's way of always coming back by nightfall. I mean we figured on that, his coming back and letting us out, so we stayed cheerful." He winced at the word. "We talked. With me, Kevin always had plenty of talk in him. And there was a bit of a stone he found in his pocket and we made games with it—target, you know, and the like. That kept us stirring about and helped to keep our minds off the cold. And Kevin, smart as he was, had us to thromp our arms about and to jump up and down against the chill.

"Even so, the cold was harsh. . . . We felt *it* more than we felt being hungry. We'd not had a proper breakfast, as you know, and Kevin"—her mouth broke in a sudden, strong smile— "along about dinnertime, Kevin put out he'd swallow a whole pot of scalding tea and eat a loaf all for himself if he but could. He set me laughing the way he said it, it was so daft. Exaggerated, I mean. . . . I'm telling you all this so you'll see how we passed the time. How we kept our spirits up all the day. . . .

"It was when it got to be late afternoon, dusk-time and after, then dark and the night full on us and our dad not come back, that we began to lose heart—though, mind, we didn't say so . . . only felt it between us. . . . Out loud, of course, we kept telling each other it'd be any minute now our dad would come. We kept *hoping*, is what I mean to say. . . .

"There was stars out; we could see them through

the breaks in the roof. Kevin said he was glad for the sight of them but I don't know, for me they were like another worry, there was such a might and pull to them, like they'd draw me out of myself. Telling of the way they made me feel sounds cracked does it, Father?"

"No, Enda dear, I've had the feeling myself."

She gave him a slight, drifted smile. "It's strange about stars. To this day I'm not sure of them."

In the light from the fire and in the candles' pale flickerings her beauty, like a scald, set a fresh mark on him. In the five years he had known her he'd never got used to the sight of her, of her deep enormous eyes, her fair skin and her hair, dark still and darker every year he could count back, with glints of rust in it, the length of it bound in a bun or braided down, or loose sometimes, flying in the wind around her face and her laughter breaking through the strands of it. . . .

"Father?"

Abashed, he looked swiftly from her, down, to his shoes. Then: "Shall you go on, Enda?"

"Aye, . . . Like I said, it was our *hope* that kept us going. That, and our listening for a sound of our dad. . . . You've seen a good dog when its master's due home, how it'll sit, all the life of it in its ears, trying to catch the hint of a footfall on the sod a mile away. . . . We were like that. I can still feel how it was, Father. How the listening took us over and carried us along all through the night.

"In time, though—it was around daybreak—we took in that it was useless to listen and hope anymore. . . . Kevin brought it up, that this might be the time our dad would never come back. He didn't forward the end for us, that we'd die, he just said, 'This might be the time he won't come back,' very quiet and set-like. I'd been thinking it of course myself, but that Kevin said it set me to crying. . . .

"You have to know, Father, that Kevin never liked me to cry. It was so from the time we were mites. Whenever I did—and I credit myself it wasn't often—but the few times I did, Kevin never spared himself till he'd got me soothed down. He'd make a clown's face, put his thumbs to his mouth and stretch his lips back to his ears, stand on his head —whatever—anything antic, you know, to make me laugh. He was good that way. Tender as a mother. So when I started crying after he said that about our dad's not coming back, he jerked right into cheering me up, said it was a foolish thing, the very idea of our dad's not turning up, him a bad penny, and I should put it straight out of my head. And furthermore—very excited he was now—furthermore, he said, when our dad *did* come back and we were loose again, we'd grab the first chance we got to run off. Leave Donegal behind us forever. South, he said we'd go, that we'd not stay about and ever again let ourselves in for another locking-up like this one. He'd been planning it, he said, our running away, how we'd get along and all, letting ourselves out as a pair, him at stable and yardwork and me indoors as helper to a cook or at laundering. It was lovely the way he told how it would be. Like a dream. . . .

"Very quieting to me, too. Made me fall asleep . . . or not what you'd exactly call asleep, for when I did stir again, it wasn't like a proper waking-up at all—fresh, you know, and on the ready—but only a slow sort of coming 'round and of feeling terrible dizzy. . . .

"There was a first bit of dawn-light beginning to show through the breaks in the roof. . . . Kevin, when I turned to him, was just as he'd been when I drifted off, sitting with his back against the door, his legs straight out before him, only now his eyes were closed so I figured him to be asleep. . . . But then"—her eyes widened and a stricken look came over her face—"I got terrible frightened over something about him, the stiff way he was sitting maybe it was, or that I couldn't hear him breathing, and I edged my way closer to him so I could see him better." Her eyes filled now with terror: "He looked—" she shuddered, "—his face and his hands—the fingers—they were the colour of set tallow, and, I don't know, I lost my head . . . went daft, I suppose you'd say . . . screamed and started in shaking, thinking he was dead—"

At this crisis-point of the past and as he intently watched at work the present mounting effects of her recollected anguish, himself in the power of her profound capacity, the cords of her neck enlarged and throbbed and her body seemed suddenly to heave itself upright and the room to fill with a strangling scream, coming from her throat.

"Enda!" he cried, brought to his feet. "Enda," stooping to her, "Swallow! Can you swallow?" taking up her half-empty cup, holding it to her lips, and, as the fluid spilled, his hand on her throat, rubbing it: "Enda, Enda," then, seeing her breast lift and heave with a rasped-in draught of air: *"Enda dear,"* his relief a moan.

She sat back, spent and, in his near, urgent look, remote; yet on his arm her hand's hold, the grip more powerful for its wordlessness: "Enda," he whispered passionately, a stranger to himself.

She caught—he saw it happen—the intense interiority of the voice he hardly recognized as his own (what had been done to him?) and instantly withdrew her hand from his arm. Then, in a distant, gathered way that sent him from her back to his chair: "I'm sorry," she said. "I thought it was laid deeper to rest in me than I see it is."

"But you're all right now?" he asked, staging matter-of-factness. "You're sure?"

"I am," she answered, regarding him from what he accepted as being her position of control; and, after a moment, "So I'll go on?"

He nodded.

"He wasn't dead of course, Kevin. . . . My screaming"—she shifted in her chair—"it jolted him. Wagged him to like he'd been jumped! So I knew he was all right. *Saw* that he was, I mean." Her brows came together in a frown of wonderment. "Rightly, knowing he was alive, I should have come out of my scare and calmed down, but—" she bent earnestly towards him: "I don't know . . . ," and to his encouraging gesture, "thank you, Father. . . . What *took* me was the other side of the coin. I mean, his *not* being dead set me to shaking worse than when I'd thought he *was*. I tried," she hastened on, "to take charge of myself. Made all the effort I could—with my *will*, as you'd say, and, you know, with my body too. Held my breath for as long as I could. Clamped my jaws to, determined. That sort of thing. . . . But the power wasn't in me." Then, as if she had a sudden inspiration: "I just thought, Father—that cousin to the Cowpers? The one that visits now and again? You see her on the street with Mrs. Cowper, every bit of her shaking?" and to his nod: "I was like her, Father."

"It was the shock of relief, Enda."

"Whatever," she murmured, "it was ruinous to

Kevin. He couldn't settle me, you see, for all his trying." Her voice dropped. "*That*—that he couldn't —made him helpless in his own eyes and"—her lips trembled—"it broke him."

"Broke him?"

"Brought him to the end of himself." Her voice was steady but barely audible: "He started crying . . . but not out loud. If it had been out loud I might have got hold of myself. But there wasn't a sound from him, just the tears on his face. Them, and hopelessness."

He thought he could not bear her visibly remembered suffering and, helplessly, near wonderingly, he examined his hands, turned them over slowly, peering at them as if there, in his own palms' lines, he might find some graven, antidotal hieroglyph of reason or comfort to offer her. Finally he said: "An ordeal like that—" and stopped himself—*is a test of faith*, is what he arrested himself from saying—and said instead: "In all my life, Enda, I've not heard of such a kind of torment."

"*Torment!*" she blurted out. "Aye, Father!" and, with a brilliant look: "You see it now, how it was with Kevin and me. How what we did, it but *happened*—"

"*What,*" he broke in imperatively.

"What?" she repeated.

"*What happened?*"

"That we took to each other," she answered with

a profound simplicity, "being all we had and thinking we were to die."

He gazed at her in a fix of sorrow and something else he could not then name. (An acute secular shyness? as he thought on it later. . . .) Whatever; with augury of her tale's bourne, towards which, outside the confessional, and against all his principles and priestly disciplines, he had allowed her to lead him. And having to know (he reasoned it his duty) and the tool of interrogation being the only one he had for mining the specificity and seriousness of the deed, he asked, as in the confessional: "What do you mean, Enda, when you say you 'took to each other'?"

Her calm gave way to a faint confusion, but her voice remained steady: "Kevin—for the comfort, Father—against the cold, like he was a blanket, he covered me with himself."

"Sexually?" Said, the syllables hung.

"Aye," she said softly, "it came to that, but not as a sin."

Not (he spoke to himself) as lust, or as an act rehearsed and wickedly anticipated in the imagination, but as a grave, countering vitality against the rot of despair. Still: " 'Not as a sin'?" he gave quietly back to her.

"As I said, things being the way they were, it but happened," she answered simply.

He nodded. Then, patiently: "Enda dear, I realize the terror and torment you and Kevin were suffering. I acknowledge the extraordinary circumstances, but what you did was nevertheless a sin and you should properly bring it to the confessional."

"You agreed!" she cut in sharply.

"I did! I grant you I did. But as a *priest* I must—"

"Then we'll quit with it," she blazed.

"Enda! *Please.* Try to understand."

But she would not be stopped: " 'Tis not as a priest I'm telling it to you."

"I appreciate—"

"—'Tis as the friend you've been to Kevin and myself."

"I understand that, Enda, but—"

"As a friend," she repeated stubbornly.

"But Enda, can you not see it?" he pressed, "That I'm *both*? Friend *and* priest. *Both*, and that I cannot divide myself—"

She gnarled her brow. "Your being a priest," she began deliberately, then gained a canny speed, "would that be the *purpose* of your being a friend?"

He shot her a glance of the most intense admiration, then, to erase it, turned from her. "As I said, I cannot divide myself," he repeated.

"But you'll hear me out? For Kevin's sake?"

He ignored her second question, replying with: "If you wish me to, and on the terms of my not dividing myself."

"It wasn't me that brought up the dividing of yourself," she brooded.

"Enda," he all but growled.

"So I'll go on." But she was scattered. She said, "I'm not sure where to pick up."

It was a positive relief to him to help her. "Your dad did come back, of course," he stated quietly.

"Oh," she instantly replied, "he did, of course."

"When?"

"Dusk-time of that afternoon." She turned her gaze to the fire. "By then—it'd been thirty-six hours for Kevin and me—we were near senseless; almost too far gone to care. . . ." Her voice deepened: "I haven't told you of one thing, Father—over and above everything else, how *thirst* got to us." Her mouth dropped bitterly. "To this day I can't think of it." She made fists of her hands. "I've no means to tell you how cruel thirst is. . . . Kevin, but a fortnight ago, sick as he was, he had his dream about it. . . . It was a regular thing with him, that dream, always the same as he'd tell it to me, that he was perishing for want of water. . . . It makes me wild to think of it."

He urged, "Don't dwell on it, Enda; it'll do no good." Then, foolishly, because she remained so pitched: "I can imagine how terrible it must have been."

She started: "No, you can't," she said abruptly, though not unkindly. "It's something that can't be imagined." Then: "But you're right, Father, that it does no good to dwell on it, all these years later especially. At the time, though, we had nought but to dwell on it. . . ."

"Go on, Enda."

She made a lifting motion with her shoulders: "Like I said, by the time our dad got back, we could hardly stir ourselves to care. . . . Earlier in the day, around noontime I guess it was, Kevin'd had a sort of fit, stood up and sawed at the air with his arms and cursed our dad, called him a bastard—begging your pardon, Father—and said how he hated him and that he'd kill him if he but could. . . . I remember the look on his face when he said about killing him. . . . Then, it was like his legs gave under him, he dropped down onto the floor and sobbed." There was, in her voice, the inflection of immeasurable distress: "His fit, and the way he caved in after it, it was a turning point for us—it fixed for us, I mean, in our hearts, that we were to die and that there was nothing left for us but to get through the lingering. In a queer way, for myself, I felt relieved. . . . I think Kevin did too, that he didn't have to put on for me anymore." She looked down, shyly, into her lap: "We hugged each other, the way you do, you know, when you're saying goodbye. Kevin said he'd pray for my soul and I told him I'd pray for his. Then we set ourselves apart, meaning to die that way, together of course as we were in the one room, but still, apart. . . ."

"Enda, my dear—"

She seemed not to have heard him: "The cold and all was so deep in us—everything—and our will to let ourselves die . . . we'd got senseless, like I said, so the fact of our dad's having come back didn't *take* with us right away. It was his ranting and kicking at things and his cursing after he'd finally got himself inside the house and the furtherance of his frenzy, knocking things about downstairs, yelling and coughing—it finally *reached* us as you might say, that he was truly back. . . . Kevin, from where he was on the floor, he whispered to me that he was going to call to our dad, that maybe he'd care to hear and come up with the key right away and let us out, but that surely, anyhow, when he sobered up a bit, he'd come up, so we weren't lost after all, and that when he *did* come up, I was to take my lead from him—"

"From Kevin, you mean?"

"Aye—to just burr myself to him, was the way he put it. Then he booted the floor hard and called out twice. . . . I was sure that drunk as our dad was, he'd not answer, but I was wrong. He bawled right back at Kevin, charging him with neglect of the fire, and where was I with his supper and so forth, bellowing loud enough to break your eardrums, and the walls that thick. . . . Kevin waited for him to take a breath, then booted the floor again and called to him that if he'd but come upstairs and unlock the door and let us out, we'd see to whatever he wanted. . . . Our dad—there wasn't a sound from him for a minute or two, but in a bit we heard him scrabbling through the tins where we kept the flour and such, stuff that spoils, you know, and as it had come on to be dark, we figured he was searching out the match-tin so he could light a wick. . . . After a while—oh, I couldn't say how long, forever, it seemed—we heard him put a foot to the stairs. Kevin told me, 'Leave him to me.' " She straightened her back: "I won't draw it out, Father, only to say that we hardly breathed all the time it took him fiddling to get the key in the lock. Being unsteady, it was a task for him. But he finally managed, and the bolt let. . . . We were standing on the ready just inside the door, and when it swung open, Kevin drove himself at our dad—knocked him off his feet—and we hared past him down the stairs. *What*, Father?"

He'd startled her by thromping his hands on the sides of his chair: "Free!" he cried exultantly, "You were *free*!"

"Aye—" she drew out the word with a rueful tongue, "we were loose all right, but still, there was little that was natural for us with things as they were, like we'd barely got to the foot of the stairs when our dad started to his feet in one of his thriving rages, threatening us with every punishment in the book. . . . The candle—there was but a single wick lit—it made a shadow of himself on the wall behind—monstrous, every part of him swollen. It was like there was two of him over us. . . . Kevin ordered me to get the axe—it was kept just inside the back door—then he faced up the stairs to our dad and told him, 'I'm in charge now.' Our dad started out of his jacket, making ready, you know, to brawl, shouting how he'd bundle Kevin once and for all, but Kevin told him 'You but try and I swear before God I'll kill you.' I'd got the axe by then and he took it from me and held it up over his head and told our dad again, 'I'll kill you.' Like *that*"—she snapped her fingers —"our dad took hold of himself. . . . People given to drink can do that, Father, as I'm sure you've noticed, get hold of themselves, far gone as they may be. Our dad, he put his hands together and asked Kevin, 'Now what kind of a thing is that to say to your own flesh and blood?' wheedling-like, his eyes very wide and surprised-looking, and his chin tilted in that crippled way he could put on. . . . But Kevin only waved the axe back at him. Then —it took me by surprise—Kevin brought me into it, telling our dad, 'Myself and Enda'll take no pity on you if you cross us.' It set me up, his saying that, that he counted us together against the worry of our dad. It shocks you, I can see, Father, that it made me proud—"

"No, Enda, you're wrong. It doesn't shock me. Believe me."

"I do if you say so."

"Go on, Enda."

"Well, then Kevin told me to get a draught of water for us, but warned me against drinking more than a bit. I knew what he meant, of course, having seen parched creatures bloat themselves. Then he told me the next thing that was needed was to get a fire going and more candles lit, and after that a bit of food laid out, only he felt, he said, that it'd be a mistake if he gave off the guarding of our dad's conduct, and could I do the necessaries by myself. 'Have you the strength?' he asked me. . . . I told him I did. I put a sweater over his shoulders and a shawl over myself and went to work. . . . The fire took in jig time and the place began to warm up. It was," she smiled dimly, "to be in the world again. Still, all the while I was working I was careful not to let go my attention of our dad, knowing him for his tricks and figuring to be ready to back up Kevin if the need came. . . . Our dad'd sprawled himself down on the bit of landing, intending you know to make himself look abused, then he started in whining about all the hardships he'd put himself through on our account and how we owed him a bit of respect for all his troubles. Maundering, you know, on and on, trying to shame us." She took a breath: "He almost got my pity with his coughing. . . . He'd bend double, hawking and spitting-up like. It make him an awful sight. . . . But he'd come out of an attack and start in again at us, saying things and—" She let the thought go. "We knew of course his ways when he'd come home after one of his sprees. The *stages*, as you might say, the meanness and the ranting, and in a while how he'd begin to get dim and heavy-like, the steam gone out of him, and all he'd want was his bed. He'd sleep then for hours, snoring so loud you could hear him in the hills. And the *smell*, Father!" she turned away.

"Drink's a terrible thing," he affirmed.

"*Terrible*," she picked up. "The lives it ruins! If people but knew when they start in on it!"

"Some know and take it up anyhow."

"It's beyond me how they can—"

He saw her face liven to the subject, and he thought for a moment she might lapse into a gossip about the drinkers in the parish, but he was wrong: without prompting, she put herself back on the track of her telling.

"Anyhow, Father, in a bit our dad got to that point where he couldn't stay awake. We saw his head lop to one side and knew it wasn't but a matter of seconds before he'd be snoring. . . . I had tea ready and some bread laid out, and Kevin said, 'Let's eat now.' Famished as we were, we still had the sense not to gorge ourselves." Again, the dim smile: "I credit us with that, that we ate like human beings in a regular way. . . . When we'd finished, Kevin whispered to me that he'd tell me now what we were to do—his 'plan,' as he put it. He started off by pointing to the mantel-board. Bright as he was—Kevin never missed anything—he'd noticed that our dad'd laid the two house-keys there. . . . We had, he said, to get some rest, for at the crack of dawn we were lighting out for good. He'd worked it through in his mind, that we'd sleep that night in the shed behind the house, only this time, he went on to say, it'd be our dad who'd be locked up—*that* so we wouldn't have the worry and fear of him while we slept. In the morning, just before we'd leave, we'd unlock the back door from the outside. We'd take nothing with us but our clothes—our warmest, he warned—and a bit of food in a pack with a jug of water and—" she drew her brows together: "there was a few coins in a cup over the sink, 'the extra,' as our dad called it. He'd always empty out the cup when we went to Mass. . . . I have to say he was good about putting the bit aside. . . . I was for not taking the money, but Kevin asked, 'Why shouldn't we?'—we'd worked ourselves raw around the place since we were small, and in that sense we'd earned it. . . . It was a pitiful sum, Father, no more than a few pence. . . . In the end, I went along with Kevin about taking it."

"I don't see that as being so wrong a thing to have done, Enda."

"*Don't* you, Father?" she asked, with an eager, gratified glance, over and back, at Kevin's body.

"There's no possible question as to your having earned the money," he said solemnly.

"So I can put to rest our taking of it, Father?"

"Indeed. . . . But tell me now, Enda dear," he urged, wanting her to continue, "Kevin's plan—I gather it worked."

"Every step of it," she answered firmly. "I stripped the settle-bed of its covers and took them out to the shed. . . . We put up a pouch of food, what was left of the bread on the table and a few tins of sardines and the like, and got together what clothes we'd wear. At the last, Kevin took the money from the cup. . . . We worked quietly, you know, but even if we hadn't, our dad wouldn't have opened an eye, he was that far out. But still, we stayed watchful of any sign of devilment from him. . . . Finally, Kevin put me through the front door and I locked it from the outside—drew down the hasp, even; then I went around to the rear door where Kevin was waiting, him having locked that door too, of course. Then we walked through the night to the shed. . . . Like I said, I'd brought out covers. . . . We piled up some straw and made a makeshift bed. Stirred up as I was, I hadn't thought I'd sleep a wink, but—" she laughed gently, "I did, *surely*, for the next thing I knew Kevin was shaking me, saying to get up, it was time we were on our way. . . . The dawn'd hardly begun to show and it was raining, *winter* rain, Father, you know, very dense and mean. Kevin spoke of the weather, said it was awful for being out in on foot, but, on the good side, it meant there'd be no way our dad could course us if he took it in his head to try. He went on to say that the instant he unlocked the back door, he wanted us to move fast. 'We'll skirt Killybegs,' he said, 'and once we've got around it, we'll head straight south.' . . . We were known a bit in Killybegs, you see, Father."

He nodded.

She made a vague movement with her hands: "Faced with leaving—I don't know—the thought of it emptied me out, and for a minute I went blank. It was like I couldn't see backwards nor forwards, if you follow me."

"I do."

"Kevin saw me teeter, but he didn't rush to right me, just shouldered the food-pouch, walked to the shed-door and opened it as wide as it'd go." She drew a hand over her brow. "I can still draw up,

Father, how he looked, standing there, braced and . . . narrow, somehow. Out for himself. *Aimed*, as you might say, and in his mind already on his way. . . . That he would go without me, Father —it was something I'd never considered." Even now, there was a tinge of awe in her voice.

"And was it that that decided you, Enda?" he asked.

She appeared not to have heard his question. "Kevin, over his shoulder, he told me, 'If you stay, it'll be the same as doing away with yourself.' " She drew a breath. "Of everything in the world he could have said to me, that was the clearest, wasn't it, Father?" She livened: "I knew right away then that I'd go and never look back. . . . I tied my shawl over my head and said I was ready now. Kevin turned around—looked very sharp at me—then gave me the loveliest smile, the kind, you know, that lives with you. . . . He was very excited, kept eyeing the house and the sky. Then, like he was on a clock, he said, 'The time's come.' He told me to stay right where I was while he went to the house to see to the unlocking of the back door. . . . I watched him make his way to it, keeping low, being careful. When he got to the door, he put his ear to it, making sure, you know, of a sound from our dad. The light was poor, but still there was enough for me to see when he set the key to the lock. Then he waved to me. That was his sign to me to take off. He wanted me to get a start, you see, before he turned the key. . . . I waved back and cut out as fast as I could in the direction we'd agreed on. The winter grass was thick and matted awful from the rain, very slippery too, and the ground so rutted I didn't dare take my eyes off it for so much as a second. Just *ran*. . . . After a bit, I heard Kevin coming up from behind. He was breathing ever so hard. When he got even with me, he grabbed my hand, encouraging me, you know, to keep going. . . . We kept at a run all the way up the first slope, not giving a thought to anything but the getting up of it. At the crown, though, we let up and I looked beyond and"—her eyes widened—"I can still feel how my heart turned over. The hills! They looked to me to stretch forever in front of us, no end to them. And—you know how mist shifts the land about, how what's there one minute isn't there the next and the way a valley'll be lost to you at the same time a mountain-top'll show itself and it not attached to the earth, how the changes leave you with the sense that there's no finish to the reaches—"

Her voice dropped. She put her head back and looked off, through the wall, far, far away, to a point, he thought, beyond distance. Her fervency of detached attention affected him in a way he had for years unaccustomed himself to, and he sat mute, in a paralysis of involvement, as might a man who hears a call from the dead and desires passionately to answer but cannot, being caught unready, and too amazed, and too glad for belief.

"Of course," she said at last, breaking the long silence, startling him, "of course, it wasn't the first time I'd been to the top of that slope, but always before I'd stopped there at the high point and but looked out over the reaches with the idea of their being beyond my range. It'd never crossed my mind, I mean, to venture further, down into the next valley and up the yon after-slope, on and on. Just knowing as I did how thick the spinneys were between the hills, so dense in places the sheep couldn't make through them, why that alone would still the notion. So the thought of us going on, that we could be that bold! Well, like I said, it made my heart turn over. . . .

"I looked to Kevin to see if he was dumbstruck too, but he wasn't. Not at all; only tugged at my hand like he was pulling me *back*, and that confused me for a second, but then he explained that now, as we were out of sight of the house, we could set a slower pace for ourselves, though *within reason*, he was careful to say, we ought to keep moving along. I asked him how long he figured we'd be at getting around Killybegs. That was the same, you see, Father, as asking him how long we'd be in the hills, only I put it that way to keep the sting out of the question. . . . He said he wasn't sure. By nightfall, did he think? I asked him. He said he hoped so, but he couldn't promise: there was too much he didn't know about how rough the going would be. But then he said there was *one* thing, though, he could tell me for *certain*: that whatever was before us, the worst was behind us! The way he said it, so *sure*, and—" she hesitated, searching in her way for just the word she wanted, "—and *sporting-like*, as is said—I can't tell you how it put the starch back into me, Father, how it made the future seem real to me again." A smile lit her face. She said shyly, alluringly, "It was thrilling."

"Indeed," he said warmly, "indeed! To think of it, the two of you so young, taking on the world like that!"

"Fifteen and fourteen!" she exclaimed in a blend of wonder and triumph, then laughed. "But as is said, Father, babes and ditherers'll take on anything." She laughed again but quietened suddenly, was soundless and still, simply sitting there as if she were alone; as if he were not present. Under her high, white brow her eyes, veiled in pensiveness, were immense.

"Enda?" he spoke at last.

She started and made a gesture with both her hands as of closing a drawer, and, straightening her back, impersonating attendance, said, "That's the all of it, Father. . . . The rest you know."

"Oh," the priest in him all but shouted, "but I don't."

She looked surprised, then—he saw it happen —*touched*, by what in his outcry she mistakenly took as a zestful yen and appeal for details of her and Kevin's adventures, and before he could put her straight—before he had a chance to collect himself and put together the track of questions he must, as her confessor, have the answers to—she, flushing with pleasure at his interest, said deeply, "Oh, Father, I could hold you here a year telling you all the particulars of what happened to us over the next months!"

And again, before he could open his mouth, she led: "We were so green, you know—hardly born, as you might say, in terms of what we knew of the world. And our having never known anybody to speak to other than ourselves, we were shy and timid as hares. But our being timid, it worked for us, kept us geared and wide-awake every second: we didn't want anything to pass us by, you see, for fear we'd miss something in the way of a lesson we could use later on. . . . The first time we found ourselves in a big crowd—we landed in Donegal Town on a Saturday morning—we couldn't believe the excitement of it, all the people moving about in the square, bent on themselves and what they were up to, paying no mind at all to us. We kept telling each other not to gawk—their clothes, you know, and their ways! And the *talk* they had in them!" She smiled broadly. "You can imagine how it was for us, Father."

He nodded, and, having made the decision to let her go on, he asked, "Did you work? Tell me how you got along."

Her face grew serious again. "It was Kevin's wits that got us through. . . . We stayed anxious about our leaving traces of ourselves, so we kept going, went from Donegal Town to Sligo, on down Calloony way, all in stages, of course, a few miles one week and a few the next. We stayed nights in the ruins of old places and sometimes in shepherds' huts; Kevin had a keen eye for ones there'd be little likelihood of our being caught in. Every few days, he'd go into whatever town we were near and ask if there was any work to be had. 'Anything for a bit of a wage,' was the way he came to put it. Saying it that way made it sound like he'd settle for the lowest figure, and as there's always somebody up to doing something, he regularly got taken on for an odd job with an end to it, carting, mending fences, whitewashing, this or that or the like, and being Kevin, he'd always do a tap more than was expected of him, so the extra penny came his way more often than not. . . . It wasn't till we got to Ballymote that we settled in for a bit."

"Oh? Tell me, Enda."

"We came on a grand place, one such as you'd see in a picture. . . . We took the morning to skirting it about. It had *rows* of out-buildings, Father, and stables, a greenhouse, too, and of course the main house, *grand*, as I said, and, well, you know, for a place like that, as Kevin let out to me, *hands* was needed. By noontime, Kevin'd made up his mind that we should go together to the gate-keeper's lodge and see if there might be work for us as a pair. If it proved out for us, he said, it'd give us a chance to catch our breath. But before we went to ask, he took off for Ballymote town and bought a curtain ring for my finger, had the part you put the thread through filed off so it'd look like a wedding ring. You can see—" She held out her left hand with the eagerness of a child showing off a treasure. "I've never had it off," she said, and, not taking in his attempt to speak: "Mid-afternoon, we got ourselves to the gate-keeper's lodge, scared half to death of course at our boldness, but hiding it as best we could. . . . There was a door open. . . . It was early on in the spring by then, and the day was a fine one, so we were seen from the inside before we could knock. It was Mrs. Cronin saw us, a nice woman she was, but of course, us being strangers, she was cautious, asked us what we wanted, eyed us, you know, as you would tinkers. Kevin, though—you wouldn't have known he had it in him—he spoke right up, said we were looking for work, that we were willing to take on anything, and might she know if help was needed on the place. I could tell she thought well of Kevin that he was so direct and all at the same time he'd taken his cap off to her. She told him the estate manager was the only one who attended to such matters, but if we cared to wait, we could sit out on the porch bench while her boy went up to ask Mr. Dunne. It was Mr. Dunne was the manager, she said. Kevin thanked her and said surely we'd wait. She went to the back of the lodge, and we heard her tell her boy to go find Mr. Dunne and ask him was he interested in seeing a pair seeking work.

"To be frank with you, Father, I didn't expect anything to come of it, but in a while a man came down the lane in a *car*, mind, and got out and told Kevin he was Mr. Dunne and what were we looking for in the way of work? We were both on our feet before him, or course, but it was Kevin did the talking, giving out to him that we'd do whatever was needed of us, that we weren't afraid of tackling any sort of honest job. Mr. Dunne was good about the way he gauged us, didn't look at us like we were sheep or anything like that. I have to say about him that he wasn't a man who'd ever set himself up in a way that'd make a person feel small. But still and all, he wasn't one for giving out something for nothing, either. He was *firm*, firm, from head to toe. Firm and up front, as Kevin put it to me later. He asked us our names and I saw him look at my hand. 'You're married?' he asked, and Kevin said we were. 'New-married?' he asked, then smiled and said he could tell we were from the look of me blushing. I was hot from the lies, from everything else too, but of course he knew none of that. 'You're how old?' he asked next, and Kevin put out he was eighteen and me seventeen. Mr. Dunne took that down without a blink. Then he told Kevin that it being a busy time of the year he could use an extra hand but he'd have to warn us, the owner of the place was very particular about workers on the place, so any shirking or misdeeds wouldn't be tolerated. Then he told us it was Sir Edward Spencer owned the place; him and Lady Charlotte. English they were, he said. He went on to say he'd have to set us up over the stables; there was an empty loft-room there, he said, and how did that sound to us? Kevin said it would suit us fine and that if we could but be given the chance, we'd not let him nor the owners down. Mr. Dunne said well, we looked to be worth the chance, that he'd give us a few days' try and then he'd 'revisit the issue.' Those were his words—I'll never forget them—that he'd 'revisit the issue' as to our staying on. Then he pointed to the car and told us 'Get in.' " She smiled. "I was already overcome by his taking us on, and of course the car!—it all but finished me. Kevin and myself, we'd never been that near to one before, let alone ride in one, and I told Mr. Dunne so, and of how the very thought of it was enough to send me up a pole! It was the excitement that made me blurt out like that. Mr. Dunne, he *looked* at me. . . . I mean, until then, he'd been mostly taken up with Kevin, but after I spoke out about the car, he seemed to *settle* on me, and then—then he turned to Kevin and told him, 'It's a pretty girl you picked for your wife.' It tore through me, his saying that. . . . Of course," she mused, "a woman always remembers her first compliment."

"Of course," he smiled. "Go on please, Enda."

"Well, Mr. Dunne told us again to get in the car. Kevin shouldered our pouches and I saw him wet his lips the way he would when he was full of dread, but, I don't know, for myself, the minute I was on the seat I couldn't wait to feel how it would be when we were off and going—*it* taking *us*, you know. The speed and all. And it was wonderful, of course. *Beyond* me to tell of! The trees—there was a great long avenue of them; beech, they were—we railed past them so fast they came together in my eyes. It put me laughing, I loved it so!

"When we stopped, I just sat, stunned, you know, not thinking of where we were or of Mr. Dunne, just gone over with the joy of the ride. Mr. Dunne, though, he brought me back, asked me, 'So you liked it, Enda?' and I told him full-hearted that I *did*, that as long as I lived I'd not forget it."

He allowed himself the image of her young and, in the confusion and charm of her excitement, radiant. He added to the image a docile afternoon sun that warmed her hair. . . .

"Father?"

"I was thinking of your pleasure in the ride," he responded hastily.

"Mr. Dunne gave me three more before we left the place," she boasted, "but that first one, well, like I said, it's beyond me to tell how I loved it."

He arched his brows: "You stayed how long on the place?"

"Near three months. . . . Mr. Dunne came to speak of Kevin as 'his other right hand.' "

"And did you work too, Enda?"

She nodded. "I started very low on the ladder, at laundering, but in a bit the housekeeper, Mrs. Bowler, a queer one, but fair enough to us girls that did our work well, she put me to being one of the cook's helpers. I never gave her cause for worry, did everything just as I was told and never raised a tongue about the hours. . . . When I say she was queer—she'd line us girls up to give us, you know, our orders for the day, and always, somewhere along the way, she'd get in a word about her notions of what she called 'one's station in life,' meaning of course *ours*, not hers. She'd a bit of a pinched face, very like a marten. Haughty. Stuck on herself, as they say." She smiled. "The *people* of the world, Father: the variety!"

"Indeed," he laughed, "variety is the right word." Then: "What caused you to leave the place, Enda?"

She frowned. "It's hard to put into words, Father. . . . It was both of us wanted finally to go, not just Kevin, you shouldn't suppose. . . . It was several things, starting with the fact of there being so many people forever at our elbows. *That*, and that all our hours and steps were spelled out for us, that we were *told*, you know, every move we were to make. And the *bells*!" she spat out the word.

"Bells?"

"All manner of them," she replied vigorously. "The one rung mornings at half-five in the stable-yard to get the men up and going and again at noon sharp for their dinner-break and again at six, six being their quitting time, and inside the house, every minute, the mistress or guests—there were parties of guests forever coming and going—setting off bells and chimes and gongs, the maids tearing up and down the staircases and through the halls seeing to the answering of a fresh summons before there'd been a chance to finish with the errand of the one before it."

"Frantic," he murmured sympathetically. "And

the other reasons you left? They'd be ones of a deeper, personal sort, I'd suppose."

She let her eyes be still in his gaze, then stated weightedly, "They were."

"Tell me, Enda."

She didn't waver: "Mostly, it was the way things that were new to us kept coming at us, no end to them, and—I don't know—after a while, it wore on us." She paused, briefly considering, then qualified with: "I have to say, I don't mean things as *things* so much; once we were shown the use of something that was new to us, its *purpose*, you know, that was that as far as we were concerned. . . . What I'm talking of had more to do with ourselves—" She fidgeted; then, in a rush: "that we were outlyers."

He let her rest on the word, until: "You see, Father, the others, they'd all been raised on the place or close by to it and, well, they were *thick*, you know, in that way people are who're known to each other right down to their socks. Some of them," she hastened on, "were even knit by blood—cousins, and the cook an aunt to the head gardener's wife—ties like that. But kin or not, like I said, they were that thick." She emphasized her point by entwining her fingers.

"Ladled from the same pot of broth, as my mother used to say."

"Aye," she nodded, unsmiling, going on: "They'd

talk, you know, on and on about what they'd done together as kids, games they'd played and how one'd tricked the other, and all manner of celebrations and affairs they'd been in on, picnics and parties and sings and dances and the like, and who'd first walked out with who when they'd got to an age to think of such things and"—she raised her chin—"Kevin and myself . . . well, you know, Father, of our childhood, its irregularities as you might say, and being from the reaches how all we'd ever known for company was ourselves and our dad—" She lifted her shoulders in a concluding way, waited, then: "The worst for us was when we'd be sitting with them, *invited* by them, and they'd go into what Kevin came to call their 'private gaggles,' when something—we'd never have the least idea what—would set them off onto wigwagging and making faces, not a word of sense having passed between them, you understand, and us sitting right there, simple to what they were going on about. . . ." Her mouth tightened: "It kept us forever awkward," she finished.

"As indeed it would," he said. Then, risking the insinuation: "It must have served to drive you and Kevin in on yourselves, closer together—"

She stayed him with a responding look that combined sorrow and futility. "Mostly," she said hollowly, "it served to hurt our pride."

"That too, of course," he said with a clumsy

repairing haste, ruing deeply the venturing which, he could tell, had damaged her belief in his understanding. Fraught, he made a movement with his hands as of erasing, then plunged on with: "They must have been curious about you and Kevin, were they not?"

"At first," she answered flatly, looking off.

"Plied you with questions, did they?"

"At first, like I said. The girls with me more than the men with Kevin."

"Naturally," touching a finger to his forehead, "they'd have wanted to know when and where you first took notice of each other, and how soon you were married after you first walked out together. That kind of thing."

She nodded.

"And?"

"And?" meeting his gaze.

"You gave them some sort of satisfaction, of course?"

"In my fashion I did."

"In your fashion, Enda?"

She stiffened and came back at him with: "That I lied to them? Is that what you're getting at with me, Father?"

"Given your circumstances, I *assume* that you lied, Enda. And please don't take that attitude with me. What I'm trying to get at is the scope of the lie. Its magnitude, its effects—"

"Oh," she mused, "I just said we'd known each other all our lives, Kevin and myself, and that our getting linked, well, that when we got old enough, it just seemed like the next thing to do. I made it sound ever so middling and dull. . . ." Her mouth lifted in a shrewd smile: "There was one girl full of airs, always peeking at herself in the glass, and she put it to me early on in front of all the others: 'What was the cut of your wedding dress?' I asked her back, 'God in heaven, where would the likes of me ever get a wedding dress?' That finished the curiosity." She laughed. "Have you ever noticed, Father, how the ordinary sets to rest a person's interest in yourself?"

At his according laughter, she made a shifting, energetic gesture and asked, "Could you tell me the time please, Father?"

He read his watch aloud to her.

"Kathleen Martin and Maeve O'Callaghan are coming on the hour with the others," she said excitedly. "Catherine McPhillemy, God keep her, got them for me."

He took in her maddening gladness at having Kathleen and Maeve to keen for Kevin. She knew—ah! he knew she knew; he'd said it from the pulpit a hundred times or more—of his disapproval of professional keeners. "Banshee lamentation," he'd labelled the practice, "that robs a wake of its true grief and turns it wild."

Had she not heard the words, or was he, as a priest, so little to her she felt no need to give him mind? And to spring it on him like this, as a fact of imminent occurrence, causing him this itch of pique, nettle that she was, sitting there before him, her excitement all unhidden, and himself cut by a blade of sudden hurt and the question as suddenly formed in his mind: *Am I, then, less to her than I would wish to be?*

"Father?" she ventured timidly. "You look struck." Her eyes, as his own met them, were soft and anxious, enormously proximate and warm. "You're all right, Father?"

"*All right?*" he surprised himself by calling out, "When I've just learned I'm to look forward to a headache and to being deafened by the howling of she-wolves?"

She hooted, "Father!" and to his astonishment let out a high peal of a girlish giggle. "Father!" and again, the alluring giggle: "What a thing to say of Kathleen and Maeve!"

"Their *baying*," covering his ears with a wild gesture (surely he'd gone crazy) and positively enjoying her delight at him as a sufferer.

"And them only wanting to keep the wake lively!" she defended through her laughter. "Father!"

And himself, then, giving over to laughter steeped in irony, for to Enda, of course (he should have known), keeners howl louder of life than of death.

He said at last, smiling, mocking despair: "Whatever's to be done with you?"

She ducked her head: "Ah now, Father—"

Then, calming: "But there's plenty of time still for you to tell me more," and, picking up: "Was Mr. Dunne surprised when you and Kevin decided to leave?"

"Oh, that he was indeed," she answered readily, her mood quieting to match his. "He offered Kevin more in wages and said he'd speak to Mrs. Bowler too about a bit more for myself, made a point of asking us if we felt we'd been wronged in any way. Kept at us, you know. But Kevin stood firm. When he saw we were bent on going, he told us he was sorry to lose us and if we ever changed our minds and decided to come back, he'd always make a place for us." She smiled proudly.

"You'd considered of course what you'd do next?"

"We had," she said definitely. "Whenever we'd the chance, we'd talked of little else."

"And?"

"Well, we had it in our hearts to be near the sea again. . . ." Her face took on a ruminative look. "That we'd grown up close by it, I don't know, it was in our blood, the smell of it and the fogs. . . . I know fogs put some people off. Take poor Eileen McCafferty now, fogs are a torment for her, nothing but ghosts in them as far as she's concerned. That's from her dad's drowning, of course. . . .

But for Kevin and myself growing up, whatever variety and lift there'd been to our days had come from the sea, the clouds blown in and the storms and fogs, and then those grand days of a bright sun and wind that'd make us feel like lambs, running and cuffing each other, nothing able to tame us, not even our dad raising his arm to us and pointing to the work still to be done. . . ." She smiled. "So we figured to move in stages southwest from Ballymote, towards the coast."

"And?" his eyes fixed on her.

"I still can tell you these forty-eight years later the main places we passed through, and myself nor Kevin not ever been back to any one of them since!"

"Tell me."

"Well, there was Tubbercurry and Swinford—Kevin caught a runaway horse for a man in Swinford and the man gave over a five-pound note to him as a reward like! Imagine! In those days, that was a fortune! And at Ballyvary, we saw a good-sized place burn to the ground. Not a thing could be done."

"That's above Castlebar, isn't it, Ballyvary?"

"Aye. . . . Now, Castlebar! We couldn't get away from there fast enough!"

"Why?"

"There'd been a bachelor murdered in his bed the night before we got there, and the place was alive with the strain of it. Us being strangers, Kevin said it was best not to linger. Kevin got the full of it from a cartwright he helped put iron-shod on the wheels of a wagon. . . ." She clucked her tongue. "Terrible, a thing like that. . . . It happens more now, murder and the like. Even on an everyday basis, over the merest things, you see tempers being let out at an awful rate, isn't it so, Father?"

"Indeed. Temper's a raw-willed thing. . . . But go on, Enda. Did you get to Westport?" he asked eagerly.

"Westport!" she beamed, "I've the loveliest memories of Westport."

"Back then," he put in hurriedly, "it was completely lovely. Now, it's a bit overrun with people and traffic. Almost too lively for a place of its size. Americans like it, and Germans. *Tourists*. . . . They change a place."

"Aye, they do. But those many years ago, like you said, it was completely lovely. . . . We were a week there, Kevin having got work with a builder. Mr. McEvilly was his name. He'd a face sewn over with purple veins, but such a nice disposition. It was him as put it to Kevin that, to his mind, the coast running out towards Roonah Quay was as beautiful as could be found anywhere in the world. It was him too that gave Kevin the *map*."

"The map?"

"Aye, I've got it still. If you'll remind me, I'll show it to you sometime."

"I'd like that." He hoped she saw how enormously pleased he was that she'd made the offer.

"Mind," she larked on, "we couldn't read, of course, but Kevin—it showed the trust he had in Mr. McEvilly—he'd ticked off all the places we'd been to, and Mr. McEvilly'd put circles around them on the map. As I said, you'll see it for yourself another time. . . . When Kevin first showed the map to me, I didn't have the wit to take it at its value. He told me, 'Look, here's where we started, here's where we've been, and here's where we are'—pointing, ever so excited. But it struck me as daft, all the days we'd trudged, the *distances*, Father, and him holding a piece of paper no bigger than a square of handkerchief, nattering on and on, telling me that what I remembered as a full day's hard walk was no more than the length of a daisy petal!"

He laughed. "Go on; go on."

"I never supposed you'd be so interested, Father." Her smile was brilliant. "Well, Mr. McEvilly'd put a big dot on the map by the place he'd told Kevin was Roonah Quay. Kevin told me, 'All that blue colour beyond the dot is the *sea*, and where that dot is is where we'll be heading.' " Her face, at this moment, took on the look of a mischievous child: "Now, Father, where the dot was on the map was the length of *several* daisy petals from where Kevin said we were standing in Westport, and when I asked him how long it'd take us to accomplish the trudge and he told me he figured three days, four days at the most, I hooted! It was then he lost patience with me." She paused.

"Don't stop, Enda!" he begged, leaning forward, drawn by her lit eyes and freshly pinkened cheeks. "Take me through to the last step!"

"Father dear, that you *care* so!" she opened out her hands to him.

The sweetness of her gathering gesture charged him through with joy. "You've netted me with your telling," he said with a rushing sense of elation and, instantly, was more conscious of himself than of her.

She gave him a smile of the purest appreciation, then took up with: "As you'd suppose he would, Kevin had us to start off the next day at first light. . . . It was an overcast kind of a morning, very cool, the wind being up and the sky filled with those thin uncertain clouds that has tails to them—"

" 'Kite-clouds,' we called them when I was a boy."

"Aye," she nodded. "Beautiful they are too, sailing so fast over your head, one after the other, racing."

He remembered lying in the grass, faced heavenward, playing at the solitary game of picking out the speediest. . . .

"That day, it was like we were tied to them, Father," she mused quietly on, "like they were pulling us along, there was such a hurry in us and no hint of tiring. . . . Usually when we were on the move, we'd speak between us of what we noticed on the way, flowers and trees, different birds and creatures and the like." She stopped; then, in a rushing way: "Did you know, Father, that Kevin fancied kestrels? Indeed. . . . Since he was very small. . . . He was forever looking up, searching them out in the sky. What always took him, he said, was the way they *sit*, so high up, you know, with an entire view of the world before them yet with nothing in the world to ransom or fetter them. . . . The morning I'm speaking of, though, he was so arrowed for Roonah Quay he was blinkered to everything but the straight of the track before him. . . . As for myself, Father"—she brought her hands together in a cupping way, as if she were holding something fragile and alive—"I was near crazy with excitement! I can't tell you!" She laughed richly: "I had this certain picture in my head of a cottage with pink dog-roses and hollyhocks at the door and a cow lying in the shade of a stand of alders and sheep grazing in a pasture that let down to cliffs and the sea beyond, and inside the cottage, a blue tea-cloth spread ready on a table. . . . It was all so clear to me, being as it was a dream of the *desiring* kind—"

He marvelled at the word she'd chosen to emphasize and nodded his head in a deep, according way.

"You do see the state I was in!" She met his gaze with luminous eyes. "Well, we went all that day, happy as larks. That night, we sheltered in a rock-set very like a cave. It was at the top of a cliff that let out over the sea. . . . It's beyond me to tell you how it stirred us, the *air*, and, at last-light, the homing seabirds letting out those cries that fill you so with the feel of your own privacy. . . . Just before he fell off to sleep, Kevin told me, 'I think we're getting near to where we belong.' There was fields of stars over us, and below us waves skurling in and breaking on the rocks in that patterned way you can count by. . . . When I said my rosary, I could hardly think for the spending of all I was feeling."

Her prowess still, he thought: unkillable, emanating from her like heat.

"Father? I'm going on too much."

"No," he protested, "no. Just the contrary." And, in the clutch of a near-forgotten sense of intimacy and concentration: "It's years since I've engaged in such close talk with anyone. It makes me—happy." He might have said "sad" if he hadn't caught himself in time, then wondered whether, for what he *had* said, she'd think him ailing.

But: "A talk of the confiding sort," she said simply, "it's not everyone a person can have it with."

As to a gift, he responded: "*Thank* you, Enda dear, thank you. . . . Go on for me, please."

"Well, the next day it was a race between the sun and us, which would be up first! We had our breakfast of biscuits and water on the road. . . . The going was harder than it'd been the day before—"

"The long slopes," he said.

"Aye, and the steep," she nodded solemnly.

"*But*," he breathed, the grandeur of the view from the impetuous coastal cliffs springing up in his mind's eye, "did you not feel like one of Kevin's kestrels eyeing the world?"

"Of course!" she affirmed. "You know, Father, before Kevin got sick, we'd take the walk to Leegans Head on a fine day and be thrilled over and above all the times we'd ever been there before. It's nothing, I mean, you can ever get used to."

"Never."

"And it's there, of course," she went on, "you'll see every kind of seabird, gulls and coots, them especially, and ducks. I've always thought for queerness, cormorants is it, the way they ride the water and circle their heads about. . . ."

"But for charm, it's curlews," he put in. "And at Leegans Head, have you noticed too, Enda, how tame the land-birds are? The tits and whinchats? I had one land on my head one day."

"No!"

"Indeed! It's the seeds of the high-growing grasses that attract them in such numbers, I read somewhere once." Then, almost shyly: "There're harebells up there too."

"Carpets of them." Her eyes gleamed.

He'd come on the violent blue of them hiking, five years ago, his first summer at Roonatellin, after putting in that particularly terrible four-year stint in a profoundly troubled district of County Louth where he'd been sent by the Bishop because, as the Bishop'd told him, "I can trust you not to mix God and the Church in with the politics of the region." Still, during the time he was there, in the lash of the terrorists' narrow-eyed hatred, two of his older parishioners had been kneed and three of the younger ones—mere youths—murdered. "You're overdue some peace," the Bishop had written at last, and sent him then to tend the flock of usual-seeming beings that was Roonatellin's.

He had never spoken, nor ever would he, except in the broadest way, of his days in County Louth.

But now, to Enda, he said, "The first summer I was here, I don't know if you remember, I wasn't in good health—"

"Of course I remember, Father. It was an ulcer wasn't it you had? Dr. Jason let it out that you did to Huey Slieve. Huey had one too, and you know Huey, he blathered it abroad faster then any decent woman would have."

The irony: himself and Huey Slieve coupled by ulcers. . . . "I was tired out, too. I don't mean to go into it"—certain he mustn't—"but I mention it because I've always thought I was cured more by the heights of Leegans Head than by Desmond Jason's doctoring."

She gave him a conspirator's grin and lapsed into brogue: "Him was a bad 'un. And us at his mercy. . . . Dr. Mansfield, now, he's of a whole other cut."

"Indeed. But," he peered at his watch, "we've gotten off your telling."

"Ah. I'll go on. . . . Kevin and myself, we started down into Roonah Valley, not knowing its name then of course, and we got about halfway down the mountain—just below that knob, you know, that sticks up over Keogh's land—when the path we were on crossed another that was a bit wider and more travelled-looking, and Kevin said it'd likely be the better one for us, so we took it. We rounded the road-bed by the stream, just as you do today, only then it wasn't the road that it is now, only a well-earthed cart-track, and there before us, set back from the track, well, there was—*this*!" She trilled out the word emotionally at the same time she flung open her arms to the four walls of her home. "Forty-eight years ago last August!"

"Jubilation!"

She laughed. "Oh, Father, such as it was!" She sat straighter, terribly intense, remembering: "A more sorrowful ruin of a place you can't imagine, the thatch rotted and caved in onto the floor in places, not a pane left to a window, raspberry bushes so snarled over the yard-wall you'd have the skin taken off you if you tried to get through them. I can still see us, the way we just stood by the wall looking at the place, our tongues in our pockets for the woe of it. Still, though, there was something about it that called to us—"

"The way it nests in its own glen, would it have been?"

"That. And the slopes behind. And the sea so close, of course. But . . . it was more the *feel* of the place, ruined even as it was"—she brought her brows together—"that in its time, it'd been a glad thing—"

"And could be again," he put in.

"Aye! That's what we said when we finally did speak, that while it was sad it'd been allowed to go so far to pieces, still, there wasn't a hint of anything unnatural about it, of a haunt or the like, you know, and how, if it was fixed up and cared for, it could be ever so wonderful again."

"Did you go into the yard then and there, or did you come back to it at a later time?"

"Oh, then and there! You couldn't have kept us from looking the place over." She drew her hand through the air. "We found the thinnest spot in the raspberry tangles. . . . The yard, though, it was but one stone-heap after another—them, and old hay-mounds beaten down by the weather, and knots of vetch and thistles. . . . The door was screened over with bolted roses, but of course, the windows being out, we just stuck our heads through the frames for a peek inside. As I said, the thatch was on the floor in places, but from one of the window-openings there was a clear view of the hearth, and that set my heart to beating faster. . . ." She leaned forward. Her eyes came together in slits: "That image, Father, I'd had of the blue tea-cloth spread on a table? Well, you'll not believe it, but for me, it was there. . . . It, and a lit fire. Not the rubble and mess, but *order*, the truth, you know, of the way it could be." She spoke the last words deeply, like a proven sibyl.

He nodded vigorously. Truly, she was marvellous. "Keep on," he urged.

"Well, it wasn't till we went full around to the back of the house that we took in the cattle-fold. . . .

We'd seen a hint of the roof of it from the front, it's slate you know, but the fold itself doesn't really show from there, so we weren't prepared for the full wonder of it."

"It 'tis a fine one. Unique of its kind," he affirmed.

She beamed. "That's the word for it, Father! *Unique*. And it's a fact that just as perfect as it is now, it was then—the walls stout, laid solid, and every stone of it dry as a bone. . . . Kevin let out a whistle over it, it charged him so. He said it was built to last a thousand years. . . . The door of it was opened in all the way, and we figured a gale'd blown it so a long while back as the hinges'd rusted to a point where there was no swing left in it. . . . Kevin ventured to walk over the sill. Have you ever noticed the sill, Father?"

"Noticed it and admired it, both. A prize beauty of a stone it is."

"Aye," she nodded in dreamy satisfaction. "Well, as I was saying, Kevin stepped over the sill and called to me over his shoulder, 'Will you look at this,' awe-struck like. I didn't know what to expect, good or bad, so I stepped fast to him. Of course, the minute I was inside I wondered he was able to talk at all, the *fineness* of it, Father! The *fittings*! Stalls and pens and hay-racks, even a saddle-tree, and turned holding-pegs set in the beams, and all along the far wall that lovely deep bench! There was a grand tinker's lantern too, hung just inside the door. Birds'd built in it; a jackdaw, likely. They'll take over anything, bold as they are." Her brows came together again: "There were cobwebs thick as fish-nets between the beams, and daubers' nests galore, and that smell bats let off that gives their presence away, and, well, all such-like as you get when a place hasn't been used for a long time, but somehow all that seemed as nought. . . . To me, what *ruled* was the mindful way the place had been left. . . . You couldn't, I mean, but see how dearly it'd been tidied and of feeling that whoever had had to leave it had suffered a regard for it that must have made the parting from it a torture."

Who did he know, other than herself, who would have said that? And with such an immediate pity as to cause now, in the wake of her perception, himself to imagine a fate-struck man separating from such a plum of a place; and to conjure the man's last, wrung look into the orderly, silent, creatureless interior, and the squaring of his shoulders before the stoical stop put on his sorrow with the putting on of his cap. . . . Kevin, surely, had bade a like, cherishing farewell to the cattle-fold.

There was a rustle of sound.

He saw that Enda had moved, had turned in her chair, and was staring at Kevin's blank, lifeless face, but in such a way as to defy a reading of her emotions. And he, in turn, as a man would at a portrait of a woman whose countenance bespoke of, if not other, then of earlier, unrealized yearnings whose resonances still could stir, stared at her with a wistfulness whose essence mystified him.

Discordantly—out of the mists—he heard her voice: "Dead faces," she said whitely, "they're all the same. . . . They don't, I mean, tell of the person as they were alive."

It was her saddest moment. He saw it in her dry eyes and in the drop of her shoulders and in the proud, vulnerable stretch of her white neck. He said, helplessly, "My dear Enda—" That was all.

Of course, right then, he should have urged her to put off the end of her telling; and he was about to do so, to suggest that now, in the time left before the mourners were due, she should rest, gather herself. . . . He'd go for a bit of a walk down the lane, give her a chance to be alone.

But she got ahead of him by speaking first, and with a commanding strength: "One thing I've learned, Father—that in this life it's best to keep the then and the now and the what's-to-be as close together in your thoughts as you can. It's when you let gaps creep in, when you separate out the intervals and dwell on them, that you can't bear the sorrow." And, as if to prove her point: "It was lingering over the first time we saw the cattle-fold that got me off."

"You're right of course about joining the pieces

of life together," he said quietly. "It's the hardest part, keeping the view whole. . . . But now, Enda dear, before the others come, would you not like a bit of time to yourself?"

He thought he detected a fleeting look of—could it be disappointment? on her face.

"Oh," she exclaimed, "I was going to tell you of Father Daniels. It was him, you know, made it possible for us to have this place." Then, hastily: "Unless you're weary at last of the sound of me voice?" lapsing again into brogue, as if in embarrassment; going on: "Thinking back over the all of it with you, Father, and telling of it—it's a dear thing for me."

"And for myself, Enda," he urged on her. "It's harmonious, is it not?" he said with a felt, tranquil warmth, engendering thereby her fine smile. "And I'm *far* from weary of the sound of your voice! And furthermore, I have to tell you, Kevin once started to give me an account of how you acquired the place, but we got interrupted by one thing or another and never got back to it."

"But that he wanted you to know! It shows how he regarded you, Father."

"He spoke *nobly* of Father Daniels."

"Ah, such a dear, good man, God rest his soul. . . . Kevin told you how we went to him?"

"He didn't give details."

"*Well,*" she said broadly, "I have to go back a bit to the afternoon we came on the place."

"*Do.*"

"Kevin and myself, we knew right away of course that we'd come onto heaven on earth. Kevin said so, the two of us standing there in the cattle-fold, 'It's for us,' he said, and I didn't even think 'So's the moon' or any such-like thing that normally comes to mind when you're face to face with something beyond your reach, just told him yes, that it was. He said, 'We'll hazard staying the night, and tomorrow we'll go straight into town and seek out the priest, find out all we can about the place.' I said yes, that was the thing to do, feeling meek on the one hand and rosy on the other. Full of hope, you know."

"Believing," he put in.

"Aye, as we both had the same fierce want, and you know what's said about moving a mountain if you have the determination."

"Go on then about Father Daniels."

"Well, we did as we'd planned, went to town first thing in the morning and straight to the church—"

"Introduced yourselves to Father Daniels," he pushed her on.

"Aye. He received us in a lovely way. Kevin did the talking of course, told of ourselves, that we were looking to settle in Roonatellin and about how we'd come onto this place and that we'd like to know about it, if it could be rented, for starters, with the understanding that we'd fix up the house. . . . When I think about it I can't to this day get over how Kevin had the wit to lay it all out as he did. And the manly way he did it, Father! Like he made it his main point of our having worked at the manor at Ballymote and the satisfaction we'd given, and said he was sure if Father Daniels cared to write Mr. Dunne, he'd get a good answer back of our characters."

"What was Father Daniels like?"

"The look and ways of him, you mean? Tall, he was, with a very broad face and sharp eyes. He had the habit of putting the tips of his fingers together while he listened to you and holding them before himself like that after you'd stopped talking, so you weren't sure how he felt about what you'd said. Not until he *parted* his hands would you have an idea what he was thinking. He didn't, I mean, ever *talk* with his fingers together like that. . . ." She sat back: "I remember after Kevin'd finished with what he had to say, how Father just kept studying him through the lace-work of his fingers—not a word out of him, me thinking we must seem like a pair of loonies to him, coming in on a morning, strangers, and going on and on about a place we'd not in all our lives known of until the day before."

"It was a daring thing to do. Arresting!" he declared with fervor.

"Funny too, Father, for after we'd sat ever so long and Father as silent as the grave, just eyeing us—us in agony—he finally let down his hands onto his desk and said, well, when he'd come awake that morning, he'd never expected such a turn to his day, but novelty was a rare and welcome thing in anyone's life, wasn't it so? and laughed in ever so hearty a way. Then he got serious and told us all he knew of the place, that it was the smallhold of a widow named Connelly who'd moved to Westport after her husband died some nine or ten years before. The widow was a cripple, he told us, that being the reason she'd not been able to stay on. At the time she left, she'd turned the place over to an agent for letting out, but over a four- or five-year period there'd been a series of bad-luck tenants, all of them booted by the agent for not having lived up to their end of the bargain. . . . In the recent years, Father said, there'd been no one near the place except the once when the widow'd showed up herself in quite a grand style with a man she'd paid to drive her out in a car from Westport. Father'd met her on that occasion. She'd come, she told him, to check on the state of the place, especially the cattle-fold, the cattle-fold having been her husband's particular concern in his lifetime. She didn't care a whit about the house, she let it be known. . . . Father said he'd gone out with her to the place and sat with her in the car while she had the driver look to the cattle-fold. She was terrible bent over, Father told us, the crippling being of that order, but she was perfectly all right in mind. . . . The next day, before she went back to Westport, she'd called 'round at the parish-house and asked Father to keep an eye on the place for her, that she'd decided against renting it again, in the belief that an empty house was better than a bad tenant. . . . She'd left him her address. He'd written her but six months ago, he told us, and had had an answer back saying she supposed the time'd come for her to think of disposing of the place, and she'd be in touch. . . . Well, Kevin asked him, What did Father think of *our* letting the place and applying the money towards buying it maybe? That bold Kevin was, drumming on with our want."

The scene, as Enda described it, was as vivid to him as any he'd ever seen at the Abbey Theatre:

—*Father Daniels seated at the old relic of a dominating desk (now his own) in the intimidatingly cheerless, damp, parish-house study.*

—*Kevin and Enda sitting opposite him, looking to him as* THE CHURCH *(Aid, Light, Comfort, Strength, Hope, etcetera, etcetera), their young eyes clear and owl-*

large, their shyness overruled by the bright spur of their fanatical want.

—Sharp-eyed Father Daniels, his heart beating a bit faster for the change, the diversion, the expressed "novelty" (as against the agonies of boredom usually suffered at the desk) of so gallimaufry a situation, and then of his having to judge (probably on a churning stomach of an undigested breakfast composed of fried this and that) the truth of the tongues of the two before him, the sincerity of their Christian-seemingness, the reality and extent of their skills, and finally deciding, *after putting to himself the question:* Why not, in the name of creation, give them their chance at their vision of Eden?

"I remember," he laughed, "Kevin telling me that all the time he was pleading your cause, his tongue'd been loose as a lark's, but then, after Father Daniels'd declared he'd undertake to write Mrs. Connelly on your behalf and that he'd take the responsibility in the meantime of giving you permission to stay on at the place, how his mouth'd slammed to like he had lockjaw!"

Enda hooted, "It's true, Father. I'm here to tell you! *Kevin!* He sat before Father mute as a stone and grey as one too! It was myself, mortified that no word of thanks came from him, that opened my mouth and started in telling Father how grateful we were and how we'd take it on as a sacred duty to see he'd never be sorry for helping us. . . .And the way the poor man looked at me, Father, as you would, you know, one of those battery-run Christmas toys they have today, seeing to when, if ever, I'd run down, I was that wrought, making up for Kevin's seeming like he'd passed out!" Her eyes took on again a canny look: "If it'd been me listening to myself and recommending ourselves as I was, I'd have got suspicious, the way you do, you know, when somebody's giving themselves out as having every virtue in the book! To think of it!" She made the beguiling gesture of hiding her face in her hands.

"Go on; go on," he said gleefully.

But she didn't speak at once, and he saw, again, a ruminative warmth kindle her eyes. "When we left Father Daniels that morning, Kevin told him —he'd got his tongue back by then—that we'd start in right away on the house, that no matter the outcome with Mrs. Connelly, at least the place wouldn't be lacking for some overdue attention. . . . I don't, though, to this day, think Father Daniels had any idea how earnest Kevin was, though he told me later he'd got a notion right away of 'the steel in Kevin's spine.' Those were his words. But I think he supposed we'd do a bit here and a bit there, Jerry-like, you know. And I surely don't think he could have imagined Kevin's doing what he did that very day—" she paused dramatically.

"Enda! You've got me on the dangle!"

"Bought a nice strong donkey, Kevin did, and a secondhand cart!"

"What?" he exploded.

"Aye," she grinned. "I thought he'd gone daft till he explained to me how we'd need the creature and cart for carrying stuff the distance from town, materials for the roof, the makings for new windows, glass and all, tools, whitewash, on and on and on. . . . We'd saved all our wages from Ballymote and of course the five-pound note the man'd given Kevin for catching the runaway horse, but still and all, it didn't add up to the beginnings of all that'd be required to cover everything. Kevin, though, he but fisted his hands and said he'd take on any and every job he could find by day and give his dawns and evenings to working on the house, that that was his plan and that was what he meant to do and there'd be nothing in the world that could stop him! I told him I'd earn too, that somehow, between the two of us, we'd bring it off. . . . It was strange, but owning a creature and having the care of it, that we'd come to that—*power*, it helped to fix us in our purpose, if you follow me."

"I do."

"Looking back, I don't see how we did it, Father. . . . The seasons were pressing on us, the fall, you know, and the winter before us, and having to make the place snug—" She shook her head. "It was bone-breaking work. . . . There was times when I thought Kevin'd collapse."

"It's mind-boggling how he did it. Yourself, too," he said in a voice which rang with admiration. "But back up a bit and tell me about your first jobs in Roonatellin; how you established yourselves."

Her eyes narrowed: "We *humbled* ourselves is how, Father—going into Roonatellin the day after we saw Father Daniels, bearing the looks that's cast on strangers, and telling anyone who'd listen that we needed work and could start that very minute. . . . Kevin got the luck. . . . It was Saturday and he noticed a back-up of creatures at the farrier's shop." She shrugged. "Nobody knows these days what you're talking about when you speak of a farrier—"

"I do."

"Aye, you're of that age, Father. But you know what I mean of the ignorance today. Now it's cars and tractors. Motors of every variety. Forty-eight years ago, though, it was a creature's four legs that was the get-about and get-done of the average man—"

He nodded, wondering if it was a worse or better fact.

"—and on a good Saturday, you'd see as many as fifteen or twenty horses and donkeys lined up at a farrier's, waiting to be shod. . . . Well, like I said, Kevin took note of the back-up, the men impatient and grumbling, standing beside their beasts, losing the best of the day, and the farrier working alone, harried, drowning in his own sweat from the heat of the forge. . . . Kevin walked straight over to him, told him his name was Kevin Dennehy and that he knew how to shoe a horse and he'd be glad to help out as it looked like an extra hand was badly needed. . . . I watched from the side. . . . Mr. Burke, Fergus Burke—he was the farrier—he told Kevin very cold-like that his assistant'd failed him that day due to illness, but pressed as he was, he'd not trust his trade to a stranger, thanks very much. All that without so much as a glance up at Kevin. . . . But Kevin just planted his feet in deeper and asked if he couldn't be allowed to take on the shoeing of a *donkey*—you know, Father, how horses has always been valued more—couldn't he take on a donkey to show the worth of his work? and before Mr. Burke could answer, a farmer back at the end of the line spoke up and said he'd gladly give over his beast to Kevin, that he wanted to get on with his day. By then, just as you'd guess, all the men were eyeing Kevin, curious—*highly* interested—to see what would happen. Mr. Burke told the farmer he'd not be held responsible for the work, but all right, he'd let Kevin use his tools on the donkey. . . . Now Father," her voice dropped to a confidential tone, "Kevin'd worked with the farrier *and* the smith at the manor in Ballymote, and both of them very particular experts I have to tell you, so Kevin knew what he was up to. And if I do say so myself, Kevin had an extra feel when it came to a beast. He could sense, I mean, was it the nervous, kicking sort or not, that kind of thing, and of course, his hands being strong and steady, he was capable of keeping a good comforting hold on the leg while he pried off the old shoe and did the cleaning of the hoof. A creature'll go wild if you get to the quick, you know, so you have to be gentle and firm at the same time, in a way the animal understands. . . . And he was *grand* at the fitting of a new shoe. I never once knew him to fault on the shape, or to tap a nail into the flesh. Proper shoeing, it's an art."

"Indeed."

"Like I said, I watched from the side, and if my lips weren't seen to be moving it didn't mean I wasn't praying!" She smiled briefly. "Kevin didn't try to *impress* Mr. Burke—to show off, I mean—just set to the job in a regular manner. I saw, though, that he was careful not to get in Mr. Burke's way or to have a tool in his hand that Mr. Burke might be reaching for. . . . He kept up a nice, soft talk with the donkey, reassuring it like, and patting its neck every now and again. . . . Every so often I saw Mr. Burke give a sly look at how Kevin was getting on, but he never said a word, not even when Kevin dropped everything to give the fire a needed tending. It wasn't until Kevin'd finished tapping in the last nail and led the donkey about checking its comfort with the new shoe that Mr. Burke finally spoke up to say it was a good job—that he could have done it *faster*, but no better. . . . The men, sure-eyed as they were, they'd watched every move Kevin'd made; they nodded to each other after Mr. Burke spoke up, and the next one in line—he had a horse—turned the lead straight over to Kevin." She raised her hands in a triumphant gesture.

"Did you not want to shout at the victory?"

"Of *course*, Father," she laughed, "but for once, I held myself in. . . ." She paused; then: "As the day wore on, Kevin loosened up with Mr. Burke and the others as they stood about—told them how he'd been on the move for months searching for a place to settle and how much Roonatellin favored his wants, it being on the sea and all, and that as far as he was concerned, it seemed to hold all the answers he was looking for in a place *if*, and of course it was a large if, if he could find enough work to keep himself afloat. Open as the skies he was. . . . Some of the men—I could tell which from their faces—some listened to what he was saying and measured him for his words; others, I could see, just tolerated the talk as a means of passing the time. But when he got around to telling of his interest in the Connelly smallhold, *all* ears pricked up, I can tell you! And when he let out with how he'd got Father Daniels' kind permission to live on the place pending word from the widow Connelly about his leasing it from her, or her selling it to him on a long-haul basis, well, there wasn't an *eye* not pinned on him, and not all of them friendly! Kevin kept on, though, open, like I said, as the skies, figuring, I guessed, to lay all his cards to view as a means of finding out what he was up against." Her mouth parted in a slight smile: "If you could have heard him, Father, how he spoke of the cattle-fold, *hymning* it as you might say as the finest one in all the land and was there a man alive, given the chance, who wouldn't work his hands off in order to call it his own. . . ."

Something in Enda's reporting of that long-ago conversation of Kevin's with Mr. Burke and the other men struck him suddenly as odd. Out of kilter, though in what way was not at once clear to him, he having allowed himself (as he told himself but a few moments later) to become so thralled in Enda's secular telling as to have totally lost sight of himself as a priest. But the felt oddness, like the distracting niggle of a thorn housed just under the skin, persisted.

"Father?"

At the sound of her voice, nethered and intense and richly compelling—whose but hers had that quality of visceral density?—he spoke her name,

"Enda!" exhaling it, as one does an "*Ahhh*" when something that was a mystery comes clear, and, in a headlong rush, barked: "Kevin, in all his talk with Mr. Burke and the others—he failed to mention your name!"

He must suddenly have looked fraught and strange, even a touch wild perhaps; her startled face caused him to suppose he must.

Had he? Shown so obviously his ecclesiastical teeth, so to speak? Revealed himself as being back on the scent of sin?

For he was, of course.

Later, despising himself, he would remember how he freshened to the inquisitor's role, how, mantled again in the dogma of purpose, he settled, as inquisitors will, deeper into his chair.

"Why?" he asked in a voice as abstractly benign as a needle, "Why did Kevin not mention your name?"

"Oh," she shrugged, "I don't know, except as men tend to cut out women when they're talking between themselves. Anyhow, they didn't know of me." And, as he remained silent and waiting: "It wasn't till the end of the day when Kevin was alone with Mr. Burke, the two of them closing down the forge, that I came forward."

"And when you came forward before Mr. Burke, how did Kevin introduce you?"

From the way her mouth tightened he knew she

was fully on to the change in him. Still, she answered promptly, "He told Mr. Burke, 'This is Enda.' "

"That's all?"

She nodded.

"And what did Mr. Burke say to you?"

"The usual," she replied with a bored briskness, "That he was pleased to meet me and how was I? The like."

"Nothing else?"

"Oh, he nattered on of how he'd taken notice of me during the day and that he figured me as being Kevin's wife. . . . Asked me if I liked Roonatellin as much as Kevin. . . . As I said, the usual."

"And did either Kevin or you make the least effort to set him straight about yourselves?"

He might as well have put the question to the wall.

"Enda?"

Her eyes strayed to the dishes set out on the table.

"Enda!" he commanded.

With a doglike obedience, she turned her gaze back on him, but she did not speak, only sat with a dog's sufferance, her eyes resting patiently on his face.

He supposed her contrite. He said, gently enough, "I'm waiting your answer."

Above her eyes, her white, translucent brow—broad as his hand were he to encase it—was smooth and cool. "If you've a charge to make against myself or Kevin," she said, "then make it, Father. But give off with the worming."

Her caustic tone had in it the overtones of a snub. That, and the hard, taunting, unwomanly way she sat now, looking at him as if he were some blackguard unworthy, as if they were somewhere other than in her home, some place of rough and dubious stimulation, *as if what mattered did not matter*, all came to a boil in him. He lost not a second, but reared hotly forward in his chair and spewed out his accusation: "Kevin *and* you, given the chance of a fresh and honest beginning, you adhered to pretending you were a married couple—"

"*Adhered?*" she interrupted with a maddening grandness, "The word's unfamiliar to me."

So that he had to tread water: "You didn't," he growled, "you *didn't*—having, as I said, the chance for a clean start, either with Father Daniels or with Mr. Burke—you didn't make your true relationship known, just committed yourselves deeper to treachery and deception."

"It was *them*," she blazed, "*them* as judged us as being married."

"As you *wanted* them to."

"As we *let* them," she corrected imperiously.

"And just what, what do you mean by that?" he bawled back at her, bracing himself for a fiery retort.

But none came. Only—after a moment—quietly: "Poor man, that you can't see it." Then, at the sight of him in pieces of frustration as he was, her eyes filled with pity and, wearily, in a pulling kind of way, she told him, "We never *said*, not *ever*, to anyone in Roonatellin that we were married. It was them as supposed we were, and we let it stand that way as being simpler for us. If we'd corrected what they'd decided about us—told them we were brother and sister—they'd have gone about trying to settle our lives for us, myself expected to *want* to marry and Kevin seen by the women as a hope, the lot of them leeching on our privacy and pecking at our freedom, busy at arranging ourselves to fit the slots of their desires. . . . Their thinking we were married," she concluded simply, "it cleared it for us to be and do as we pleased."

He heard her, understood her, but, God forgive him, in the state she'd got him in of feeling demeaned and pocked as an object of her pity, and in the grip of some heretofore unknown brand of a crazed and crazy pride which imperatively and absolutely required that he recoup his dignity and score, he bludgeoned her with: "And what exactly, *outside the usual*, did it please you to be and do?"

Disbelief—no, dismay of the deepest sort arrested her features, but, like a feral dog after a lamb, he was not to be stopped. "Tell me," he insinuated, "was it the other part?" Then, crudely, "The sexual part that—"

He never finished.

She rose before him like a pillar of fire. "You could think that?" she cried, "Of Kevin and myself? That we kept it up? *Shame!*"

"I must know!" he raged. " 'Tis my duty!"

"Then God damn your duty for the filthy thing it is."

He welcomed the force of the lash as being deserved.

Despairing, he saw the twist of contempt on her face and the tears which blazoned her eyes. "You've laid a wound on me," she said; then turned from him with: "I've things to do."

Of course she had, he thought distantly: any minute now everyone would be arriving.

In a voice fractured by grief, he said, "Allow me to help—"

Her answer, made with her back to him, was tersely excluding: "It's faster done alone."

Near smothering in sorrow and self-disgust, he sat and watched her as she built up the fire and got some lamps going and rearranged the plates on the table. At the last, at each corner of the bed, she lit a fresh candle, holding the wick of the new to the flame of the feebler old. In the brighter light, Kevin's face shone whiter, moon-like, yondered truly.

There was the sound of an approaching car.

She went to the window. Peering out, her profile as it was seen against the harsh yellow beam of the nearing headlights was eyeless and black, as futile for its tellingness as a penny-purchased silhouette.

"It's the first of them coming," he said hollowly, a fool at the obvious. Aching, he stood up. He smoothed his hair with his hands. He drew a chair—could it be as heavy as it felt?—to the foot of the bed. He said, "Sit here, Enda. It's your rightful place."

She came at once and sat down.

He reached for his overcoat.

"You're not *going*?" she asked.

"I don't see how you could want me to stay."

"It wouldn't be proper for you to go." She made the reply as an admonitory fact.

"Would you have me then at the door?"

"If you will, please," she answered formally.

Now, from the yard, voices were heard, and from down the lane, a further succession of car lights showed.

He crossed the room.

He put his hand to the latch.

He said, "Forgive me if you can."

Then he lifted the latch and swung open the door and called out gently into the night, "Come in; come in. . . . Enda is waiting."

Ten

ONCE, IN THE afternoon, as he was working the bottom stretch of the beat, he looked back and saw the ruin he'd left in the wake of his day's efforts: there, all along the bosky rim and reach of the river, the crushed heather, the trampled furze, the flattened sedge: havoc of desiring.

But here now! (Might as well get a sermon out of it.) Every decent-hearted angler knows that tomorrow's rewards are kindled by today's disappointments. So to the sure-to-come "poor fool" look Seamus would cast upon him and to Thomas's "I-told-you-so" blatherings, he'd give his answer: "Another time, Seamus"; "Next season, Thomas. I'm telling you now to write it down that I'll want a beat the first Saturday of the next season." (That to go in the sermon, too: a specified time-avowal of renewed undertaking.) Repeat it: "So mark it down, Thomas. Next spring, the first Saturday of the new season. And gratitude to God for the future chance. . . ."

That moment yesterday, after Kevin's burial, still beside the new mound of the grave, Enda's whispering to him, "Will you drive me home please, Father?" and, to his answering nod, her moving closer to him, indicating that way to the lingering others she was in his care. The mourners then, seeing they had done all they could, began to drift off, back to their cars and the main road of their suspended lives. Left, then, beneath the cloud-thronged sky, he and Enda stood alone. . . .

In the aftermath of the hellish scene he'd created with her, he had done naught but review his life in terms of the crime he had committed against her. It was one of his frequent, impassioned mulls from the pulpit: *To work one's imagination on someone else is evil.*

More than his humiliation, greater than his self-loathing, profounder than the scourge of remorse, had been the pain of the ceaseless image of himself as she must see him—as a weaseling priest on the cheap.

The day after the wake—that would be but the day before yesterday—he had gone in his agony to see her but had found her in a surround of keeping women so thick she had not been able even to stand when he entered the door, that close they were around her, their feet and legs twined spiderlike beneath them, their hands busy with their teacups, their tongues working in comparing ways over other losses, other deaths. Caught in this cosseting, funereal web, she appeared blind to his presence. Catherine McPhillemy had delegated herself to fuss over him. He had stayed, hardly speaking, but a few minutes.

. . . But yesterday, together at Kevin's grave, all had been different. . . . They had stood silently, unmoving, statues among crosses, until Enda, coming to life, had lifted her hands to her throat and slowly untied the knot of the black woollen shawl that covered her head, putting to flight in the risen, capricious wind those unruly strands of hair which a heavy rope of braiding could not contain. Fully exposed, her face in the cloud-cast lavender light was marvellously beautiful. Looking at her—he could not but honestly look at her, especially in his anguish—he retreated into a memory of himself as a young, uncommitted man who, in a large book not his own, had gazed at the photograph of a found, autochthonous, terribly telling, carved, stone visage of a woman from a fargone time, and had been filled with a first flaying sense of his life fleeing from him in an unequal chase.

"You look done in," she prompted him gently.

Mired in sorrow, he answered, "I am."

As a supplicant, he took her having provided him with the chance to say so as a kindness. Given the grace of it, he was incapable, though, of putting it to use: all in a moment, the vitality of his active regret had given way to a deadly listlessness: What could he care of the present when his future, like his trodden past, would yield naught but nullity? The nearby twisted, stippled thorn-tree (Kevin's coffin was earthed deeper than its roots) was as himself.

She had tracked his gaze. "You wonder it can live," she said wanly. And when he did not respond: "About yesterday, when you came—that we couldn't talk—"

Emptied of the energy to care, he made an interrupting, dismissing gesture: "It doesn't matter."

"But it does," she said. "As between us, it does." Then, with a fervent, equalizing candour: "We've need of one another."

At her words, he suffered the immediate mix of the rescued: shyness; want of confidence; awe at deliverance; relief; speechlessness; trembling. In his thumb's grip, the bible he held seesawed wildly.

She searched him with her eyes. She took a step closer to him—began a gesture, checked it, then completed it: touched his face with her hand and spread across the flesh of his cheek the moisture of a tear.

A sudden gust of wind ballooned out the length of his vestments. "You'll take a chill," she said.

He had found his handkerchief. "You too," he told her, wiping his eyes.

"So we'd best be on our way," she answered.

"Enda—" he began, but, in a new rise of emotion, faltered.

She shook her head. "We'll not talk more of it," she said firmly.

"I must—" he told her.

"No." She stooped and snapped off a twig of heather and placed it on Kevin's grave. "Come now," she said.

They walked slowly, descending the cemetery hillside carefully, skirting headstones and crosses and clumps of gorse. The sheep that earlier, timid of the mourners, had skittered away were straggling back, grazing again.

"*Them,*" she spoke with a tender tolerance, "they don't know."

On the level ground of the road, he opened the car door for her, then went around to his side and took his place in the driver's seat. He started the engine and set the car in motion.

"If I were younger, I'd learn to drive one of these," she said. "But it's too late now. . . . Besides, it'd be a waste, Kevin having got that three-speed bike for me but a year ago."

After that they spoke no more until he made the turn off the main road onto the valley lane leading to her house. Halfway down it, he told her, "I'm going salmon fishing tomorrow. It's the last day of the season."

"You only chance then."

He nodded.

At her house, she let herself out of the car. The wind got at her hair again. She told him, "I'll be at early Mass Sunday as usual. And tomorrow, Father, you'll surely have the luck at your fishing."

He'd not turned off the engine. "I mean to try," he mustered.

She placed the car door against its clasp, then put her thigh to it, that way to close it as gently as possible.

In the rearview mirror he saw her, standing and waving, watching him out of sight.

Eleven

FIVE O'CLOCK: ONLY half an hour left before half-five, half-five being the hour he'd set for himself for quitting the beat and going back to the Castle to account. Folly, to suffer out the full time. No question, though, that he would: go on casting; go on desiring. Nothing to be done about the desiring, whitely chastened now though it was. Every aspect of every minute of the entire day—rain without surcease spilling out of the black and liquid sky; sloughed, fierce sweeps of wind; the swollen, silt-ridden, ever-swiftening river; the torturing midges; the ghosting mists like amorphous shifts of sorrow—all had acted in perfect scheme to chasten desire. Nought, though, can ever fully dry the angler's heart of it.

Why not then the Hairy Mary? Nothing would come of it, but were Seamus to bring it up as an "if only," he'd be able honestly to silence him. In the course of the afternoon, given the hopeless conditions, he'd tried a range of lures, selecting them almost solely on the basis of their fluke value: Black Fairy, Abbey, Night Hawk, Silver Wilkinson, Warden's Worry. . . . So really, at last, why not the Hairy Mary?

Bending to shelter it from the rain, he opened the fine, fleece-lined fly-case he wryly called the Declan de Loughry Treasury, the title appropriate for its containing the bulk of his worldly wealth, the exotically beautiful, delicate simulations of insecta and hexapoda being expensive—*dear*, to the point of a gasp—especially to a priest whose monetary worth was what you might elegantly describe as being the polar opposite of opulent. . . .

Ah—the Hairy Mary, nested in the fleece, just where it ought to be. . . . So tie it on, then walk back to the top of the beat and fish again the glide between the banks.

Trekking the lengthy distance back to the glide, he looked up once from the slippery shoreline and saw a kestrel sitting in the drench of the sky and thought of Kevin—of his tame, envying fondness for the wild, unlimited creature. The bird lingered above him, watching, interested: Ariel observing Caliban. . . . The notion bestowed on him for the first time that day a sense of relationship to the immutable in nature, and, in the soothe of the perspective, he felt himself growing calm.

At the glide, he decided to use as his casting-stand a ledge known locally as Gorham's Rock, a Mr. Timothy Gorham having made a kill from there some forty years before of a thirty-three-pound salmon, immortalizing himself and the rock thereby. . . . Mr. Gorham hadn't achieved the kill in these conditions, however, legend having it that there'd been just enough of an east wind to ripple the water, not this gale; and the water just high and cool enough, not this boisterous torrent and freezing water; and the water coloured like fine beer, not clouded by silt and ridden with torn, suspended matter. He caught himself at his further maundering: it was, he knew, a way of preparing himself for final defeat. But, not wishing to dishonour the memory of Timothy Gorham, he determined to put his back into his last casts, and *did*, throwing out and stripping in again and again, wholeheartedly, in the way of a foolish, committed abider.

At half-five, though, his stomach muscles aching like he'd been fisted to the ground, and his teeth clapping together like castanets—he was that frozen—he reeled in, enough being enough, and hooked the Hairy Mary into the holding-ring at the base of his rod.

He'd go now, having given it his best.

But just as he turned from the river, the already stinging rain freshened in force to a bulletlike ferocity that sent him at a trot to the questionable cover of a low-branched, exorbitantly-leafed wych elm tree. Wet completely as he already was, he might have just slogged through the spate straight to the snug of the ghillie hut, no tree being able to be more than a leaky umbrella, but the truth was he'd rather be alone and drowning than suffer the time in the hut with Seamus, for sure as could be, Seamus'd not walk from the hut to the car in such a downpour. He could all but hear Seamus's whine: "Hold a bit, Father! Surely, *now* you can spare yourself a further soaking. . . ." and so on.

Better under the tree, captive to a memory of himself on a fair morning but three years ago, resting, out of the sun, under these very branches, after making the kill of a fine twelve-pound salmon. Frank Seldon had been his ghillie then, a jewel of a man in his mid-eighties, with a soft, companionable, lyrical tongue and a godlike skill with the rod. Frank: dead now. . . . And the likes of Seamus being let out by Thomas under the guise of being a ghillie. . . .

It was because of that affectionate memory of Frank that he decided to take off the Hairy Mary and to tie on in its place (it was an utterly whimsical choice) a Size 12 Connemara Black, Frank having told him once that at the end of a fruitless day on the river, he never walked away from the beat with a lure of defeat still on his line. "It's a superstition with me," he'd added, "my hold on tomorrow." Then, with a crooked smile: "At my age, you know, you're prey to such notions."

So—and—as he'd chosen to put the time in under the tree, he'd heed Frank's words.

It was after he'd made the change of the lure and as he lingered, shivering, in a kind of mindless, melancholy trance that the fact (it was *as* a fact that he later came to speak of it)—that the *fact* of the cove which lay hard by to his right intruded itself on his consciousness as being *not* what it usually was—a mere nuisance of trespass to the angler—but a veritable lake, excessively flooded, *deep*, with waves curling its surface and at its neck, the river waters, riled to foam, still roisteringly sluicing into it.

Normally, he'd not have given the cove a second thought except for its being a sad, exaggerated, golly-fault of the spate conditions—no place, surely, where a salmon might shelter—*but*, and here again, fillip-like, another mad whim seized him: Why not, as he'd thrashed, daylong, the river to ribbons—*why not* change the locale of the whipping? And *why not*, with the Size 12 Connemara Black (madness heaped on madness) perform one cast—*only one*—into the virgin waters of the cove?

He glanced at his watch. Five-forty-three, and the rain letting up a bit. . . .

Not quite believing he was doing it, he walked resolutely from the tree and took a position at a point midway between the cove's throat and the beginning curve of its ending banks.

An hour later, back at the Castle, hemmed in by an envying press of other, end-of-the-day, fatigued, failed, whiskey-drinking anglers and their ghillies, and under urgent pressure from them as they toasted him (oh, sweet triumph) to recount every single this-and-that living particular of his kill, he'd insistently told them that *truly*, he had no notion, no idea, *really*, whatever in the world had made him go for that one last cast, knowing as he did the hopeless odds of the conditions and the million-to-one chance of a salmon's electing the cove as its lie and the ludicrous fact of the Size 12 Connemara Black lure—*yes!* a *trout* fly; imagine!—and then, just as he was about to perform the cast, to add to the folly of the exercise, the wind's devilish turnabout from giving off those even, combing sighs out of the northwest and spitting itself out instead in short, erratic, tigerish eruptions that raked and clawed the surface waters of the cove, turning it into a chaos of tiny, spiky ricks and cones and making it absolutely impossible to gauge the thrust-value of a cast, so he'd *almost* not made the cast at all, being sopped through as he was and chilled to the very marrow of his bones and paining with exhaustion and feeling he couldn't cope with a backlashed line, the damnable snarl of it to be undone, and, well, truth to tell, repeating, between the stacked odds against a decent cast and the daft fact of the cove and the Connemara Black, he'd all but decided *not* to make the cast but then was overwhelmed by the thought that he *should*, that he *ought* to, that he *must!*—as if it were a sacred duty—so *had*; though, honestly, he had to confess, he hadn't really exerted himself, not *tried*, so to speak, just raised his rod near casual-like, hardly intending, and made the fling.

And of course, just as you'd expect, it was a poor thing, falling short for lack of spirit, *yet*—and here again, the mystery of it!—bad as it was, the *presentation was excellent*, the line uncurling beautifully and the Connemara Black touching down on the water in as soft and lifelike a way as ever you could imagine or dream of.

Instantly—yes, *instantly*—the fish showed itself in a head-and-tail rise. And, of course, the spank of its action, so sudden and smarting, and him so lulled, he all but had a heart attack! And the wrist being the villain in a situation like that, he jerked the rod upwards—reflex of surprise—but, God be praised! there was sufficient slack in the line so that the Connemara Black wasn't disturbed in its watery rest. So: slowly, *slowly*, near dying, he began the tease of the strip-in.

When the beast did finally take, it wasn't a clean, enthusiastic, definite strike. Nothing like that. Rather, it took from below, almost stealthily, after, he supposed, nudging the lure with its nose, then deciding. But, *yes*, he knew well enough it was on: in its first alarm it did a complete in-place roll, causing a sign on the water and himself to have the sensation of the rod's thickening in his hand. Keen to the nuance of that sensation, he nerved himself against doing anything hasty: let the creature have its moment to turn away—worth about eight yards off the reel—before performing that deft, precise, tautening skyward lift of the rod and applying, at the same instant, the reel's check, the joint action of which, then or never, sets the hook firmly in the tough jaw of the angering salmon. "Of course. *Of course*, man!" he bawled impatiently to the big-jowled Welshman, that action supposes a larger *salmon* fly, *never*, that is to say *not*, *not* a Connemara Black with its tiny Size 12 barb meant for the more sensitive mouth of a sea-trout! So forget the fact of the Connemara Black and apply to the kill as usual. "There being no alternative," withering the Welshman with the obvious.

Understand: the flooded cove—site of the struggle—presented another hazard to the mix of the drama, for while he knew as well as he did the inside of his pocket the underwater terrain of the riverbed, he knew *nought, nought* of the cove's bottom, the location of stick-clumps, or nested, raw-edged rock-clumps, or how far out into the heavy, muddy waters the reed-beds grow, all such places being the natural refuge a fish would run for, there to tangle the line and break free of it. So the task of *controlling* the beast as he played it had been especially tricky. . . .

"It took how long?" one of the Americans asked.

"Just over thirty-five minutes." And . . . until well near the end, the only way he'd been able to handle the beast, in the controlling sense, was by maintaining an exceptionally high, above-the-head hold of his rod—a criminal position for the necessary amount of reeling in of the line and the letting out of it, the creature being a fighter with the strength of Satan (it twice bent the rod to a sure-seeming breaking point)—and him all the while with his fingers going numb for want of blood getting to them and his arms nearly torn from their sockets each and every time he slipped the check on the reel. And: "Raw, is it?" sticking out his tongue for Thomas to inspect, "Bitten to ribbons?"

Thomas knew he was a "mouther" when he played a fish.

Very near the end there'd been a hot, thorough moment when he feared he'd lost it, it so suddenly stopped rampaging. . . . *Stilled* itself, and in a way that caused the line to slacken and the tip of the rod to lift, not straight up—oh God, not *that* much!—but enough to cause him to miss a breath before he felt a verifying tug. A *tug*, mind. Not a feisty yank of renewed strength. Just a tug of the dull, heavy sort. . . .

"Poundage and fatigue," glint-eyed Thomas cut in. "And I'll wager you were glad enough then to have Seamus at your side, were you not?" lifting his shoulder importantly and blathering confidentially on to the circle: "When he 'phoned me yesterday, Father said he'd not need a ghillie. . . . But you can see for yourselves with Father's kill—the very *size* of it—the *sense* of the Castle's rule of a ghillie for every beat, and how it falls on me to see to the rule's being carried out."

"To your health, Thomas."

"*Well*, Father?"

"Well, Thomas?"

"Well, were you not glad to have Seamus?"

"Well . . . yes. Seamus waded out for the netting. . . ."

No point in publicly telling what a mess Seamus had made of the netting; that, far from being at hand and on the ready, it had taken five celestial bawlings of his name before he'd come at a walk through the rain from the ghillie hut, and without the net, a path he'd retraced at a hare's pitch once he took in why he'd been called. . . . The net retrieved, the boy had proved ignorant to the necessity of a weight for it: "A *rock*, Seamus! You call yourself a ghillie? No!—the bigger one. *That* one, for the love of God! PUT IT IN THE NET! . . . To hold it down in the water's 'what's for'!"—this last growled exasperation shattering the concentrate of silence which normally queens the final tenses of a kill. . . .

Nor how, then, as the fish surfaced and was marvellously seen, agleam, there'd been the need to instruct Seamus: "Wade out, boy! *Wade out!* I daren't bring it closer," which words, hissed forth, sent Seamus, all glory of purpose, into the water; but, his obeying haste being of the reckless sort, he'd not (of course) considered his footing, so had slipped (of course), and, careening, his head on the wobble, his mouth in the twist of an oath, his arms angled out stick-and-scarecrow-like, though (credit him) his hand maintaining its grip on the net, he was, for one bizarre moment, valued as being the living incarnation of O'Callaghan's immortal painting of "The Wounded Soldier-Boy A-Dying in the Foss." . . .

Until, as and when, *somehow*, he recovered himself, *stood*, upright and waist-high in the water, grinning in the full way of an ape, *until*—until Declan de Loughry's hurled wrath hit him, at which point his face went pale with surprise and terror: "I'm warning you, Seamus, if due to your skill as a so-called ghillie I lose this fish, I'll murder you! Now listen hard, boy. . . . I'll make a last draw-in, and when the fish shows itself again, get under it with the net. *Under* it. *And from behind*, understand? . . . Make a deep scoop with a *strong hold*. *Gear* yourself, Seamus!"—*that* order barrelled out: *it*: after which, in ultimate opposing determination, angler and fish strained, in their apartness, fatefully together.

Gleam of belly.

"*Now*, Seamus! For the love of God, NOW!"

Thus the netting; thus the kill landed.

And then, as is in clean haste done, the angler's hammer applied to the critical center of the creature's brain: one tap.

Removed from the net, it lay in the drenched fern.

It was a cock-salmon, sovereign of years, with a kype the seeming size of a walrus's tooth.

In a hush, Seamus said, "There's been none taken this season to equal it." Then: "You look near fainting, Father."

"*Do* I, Seamus? Well, if you want the truth, I'll tell you: were a leaf to fall on me now, it'd knock me over for all the strength I've left in me!" He laughed. "My God, the size of it!"

(Thomas weighed it in at a stunning twenty-four pounds, ten ounces. "And now, Father, if you'll just hold it, I'll take a flash-shot—strictly for the Castle's records, understand."

It never occurred to him that Thomas would send the developed picture, along with the negative, to the *Irish Times*, and that they would print it five days later, large as life so to speak, for all the world to see, provoking thereby that later note from the Bishop: "Nice to have you the object of such sporting notoriety. Put a bit aside in the freeze against my next visit. I'll bring the wine. . . .")

Twelve

NOTHING EXAGGERATES A sense of lonely solitude so much as a long night drive through thrashing rain and dense, culprit fog.

Crouched over the steering-wheel of the old Ford, his head thrust forward, turtle-like, out of his collar, the only sound the sidelong loping strokes of the windshield wipers, he peered ahead through the car lights' gauzy beam at the narrow, winding road which kept vanishing and reappearing like a dark ribbon in a magician's hand, seen now, now not, depending on the shift of the fog. . . .

It was terrible the way his splendid excitement had vanished almost the instant he'd left the Castle and started the homeward journey, the lilt and thrill of his great adventure draining from him suddenly, to be as suddenly replaced by a violent flush of self-pity caused (admit it) by the sorrowful fact that at the end of the long night drive there would be nought for him but the bulk emptiness of the bleak parish-house, its outside walls bleeding with damp, its windows dark, its high, cold rooms devoid of life except as he would enter them only to encounter, going before him in the chilly chambers, the exhaled, ghostly haze of his own breath; that . . . deadliness, juxtaposed to the powerful vividness of its imagined opposite: anticipation—of a lit window, of a waiting presence, of a voice asking those simple, linking, engaging questions which absence inspires: "How are you?" "How did you fare?" "What was it like?"

Oh, the blanknesses of solitude. . . .

He ought to get a dog, a lively, sensitive puppy he could rear to companionable habits; one that would accompany him on walks and ride beside him in the car, that would sleep next to his bed and wag him awake of a morning, a warm, affectionate, entertaining little dog. He pictured the creature: a smallish terrier, a brindled, charming cairn or smooth-coated brown-and-white Jack Russell, all spiff and prance and independence but ready ever for a petting. "Father Declan's little dog," mothers would say of it in a recommending way, meaning it wouldn't snap when their children stooped to pat it. " 'Tis Father Declan's": assurance that it wouldn't forget itself and spot the carpet. . . . Was there anything written against a priest having a dog? For sure the Bishop didn't have one. Could he think of a sixtyish priest he knew who did? He couldn't; though Father Patrick Joyce in Galway kept a toothless, stiff, off-putting thing of a cat, a feature of parish-house life you'd be less surprised by in Galway than in Roonatellin, priests in Galway being laws unto themselves. . . . And of course, there was the obstacle of Mrs. Duggin, who "did" for him as hasty morning-cleaner and washer and (hastier) cook. (He'd try again hinting to her how much he'd appreciate a bit of noontime meat or fish not fried to the consistency of cement, or a veg not boiled to a rag's limpness.) Mrs. Duggin wouldn't take to a dog. . . . He could hear her: "I'm hoovering *hairs*, Father, *dog* hairs," tousling the thin of her own, her mouth dropped disapprovingly. "It's not that I'm complaining of the work, the amount of it, but *dog* hairs—"

But must he forever give in to the Mrs. Duggins of the world? forever keep sublimating wishes? as he was this instant sublimating (*burying*, or trying to) the wish (he struck the word *desire*) to share with someone this singular-in-his-life, brilliantly prodigious, gallimaufry twenty-four-pound-ten-ounce day, the bodily fact of it residing in the car's boot, causing now that worrisome, unhealthy, grinding sound the engine was making (or so, in his angler's pride, he fancied the source of the noise to be). . . .

Innocent, the mere wishing of a mere wish.

The snare—face it—was the wish's hub, the core-specific: Enda.

His thoughts rested, sunning, on her name, but not for long, the thorn to such repose being guilt. Given his calling, no mortal figure should pose such allure of pleasure and affinity. . . . That he could even *think* along such lines! That he could ever *feel* so! . . . He'd end up in one of those quiet, endlessly-corridored church-run clinics for eejit ecclesiastics—as happened in that case there'd been whispers of of a priest down near Limerick who'd not shown himself for Mass, then been found locked in the bathroom, muttering to himself, his ritual-robes scissored to bits and lying in a heap at his feet. . . . And what form of scissoring would his own aberrancy take before he'd be collected and confined and put to some form of hand-busying therapy—basket-work or counting out potatoes for the noon soup—and when he was better, "coming along," and could stand the responsibility, watering the potted plants set about in the cloister. . . .

Resist.

Priestliness performed the thought of the world.

He said it aloud—"*Resist*"—then decided, *chung!* justlikethat, not to.

The ease of it! The lack of struggle! No violent, fanged, explosive impulsion of will—just the determination that this once, at the end of this day of days, he would do what he wished to do. . . .

. . . *if* he'd be but *able* to, the damnable fog being a kingly thwarter; *it*, plus the rain and the hap of road-flooding in the Maam Valley lowlands, or rock-slides, or some worse, weirder handicap, such a night being a perfect prescription for all sorts of calamitous, cantrip-like irregularities. . . .

With the best of luck, he calculated the trip would still be a donkey-slow two hours. And supposing he could—did—make it in that time, would there be (ah, the critical question!), at half-nine, a lamp still lit in Enda's window?

So risk a greater speed; hazard the curves and ditches!

Go it!

Miraculously, he had to stop but once, for a pure-white cow lying in the middle of the narrow road. With the bumper almost touching it, he was obliged to honk it to its feet. Standing, after its clumsy rise, it faced the car and stared at it, opponent-like, a there-to-stay, drenched, slathering, ton-weight hulk. What a face! The wet and slippery smear and sprawl of its nose, the length and thick of its snowy lashes, its great, certain eyes, its lifted, pink-lined ears set on the far extremes of its wide brow, the brow itself so densely unpromising, so very terribly unpromising. . . . He laughed. He lowered the window and spoke to it through the rain: "Get on now. *Move*. . . . There's a dear." But it stood, massively unheeding. He applied again the brash of the horn. . . . The creature lingered over a last, solid stare before moving at a slow walk away, its sashaying rump telling of disdain. He watched it cross the gully and go on into the close-lying field, the milk of its mythic hide luminous against the black turf. Then—the work of a moment's change—the mists, active as moths' wings, enfolded and absorbed it: gone.

He blinked, guessing at it, immense and spirit-like, traversing the yon, unseeable terrain.

The stopping for it would be something else to share with Enda.

It was a bit before half-nine when he turned from the road onto the lane that wound down the hill towards the sea: towards Enda's house. If her lamp was still lit, he'd toot the horn; its sound would bring her to the door. If the place was dark, he'd simply go by. . . .

Just after he made the turn into the lane, the rain stopped, abruptly, as it can, like a turned-off faucet. He let the window down and received gratefully a sea-blown draught of fresh air that smelled of brine and distance. The moon and the stars, he reckoned, would be out in a few minutes.

He drove as slowly as possible now, electing the

pace for its quietness and for the sake of the car's underside, the trough-like lane-bed having been gutted to a worse-than-usual state by the storm's wash. Three drowsing sheep started and scattered. Before him, between the dripping hedgerows, drowned and dropped fuchsia flowers carpeted the way in scarlet. Some distance before Catherine McPhillemy's, he dimmed the headlights and rested his foot on the brake: her collie might show itself, crouched, for a nip at the tyres. But he passed without so much as a bark, the dog, like Catherine's house, being closed up for the night.

Enda's house, he supposed with a sink of his heart, would be alike: dark; shut and still.

His mind tripped then on the memory of it having been but yesterday—only yesterday!—he'd driven in a retreating way up the lane in the opposite direction. But that had been *after*. After so much: after Kevin's death; after Enda's revelations of Kevin and herself; after the provoke and claw of his sin against her; after Kevin's funeral Mass and burial; after Enda's tacit forgiveness of him in the witnessing, powerful surround of the cemetery; after . . . *Afters* to do with the past. And now, had he come to the point of the poet's final, crucially cresting wave when the future begins, after?

He felt so.

Yet, at the sight of the yellow lamplight coming

from her window, his blood thickened in confusion: he fain would flee.

But, vagrantly, his hand betrayed him: twice—in two spurts—the car horn sounded.

He had never experienced difficulty in leaving people; farewells, being part of a larger plan, had never troubled him. Now, in an anxious torment, he could hardly stand the wait of being greeted.

She opened the door and peered out into the night.

"Enda," he called.

"Father!" She waved, then grabbed her shawl from its peg by the door and came running. "Father—"

He had opened the car door but remained seated inside.

"Enda—"

She stood at his side, close, her eyes as large and liquid as the rainwater pooled in the yard's stone-beds, her dark hair loosened like an increase of the scented night.

He felt as jumbled as a bag of rags. "If there'd not been a light showing I'd not have honked," he began in a clumsy rush, "but as there was—" pausing to catch at a straw of reason: "I'm just getting back from the fishing. . . . And you, Enda, you're all right, are you?" his eyes on her as if she were a lesson to be memorized.

She nodded.

"I wanted to make sure," he went on. "It's hard for you, I know, being alone—"

"Oh," she answered, her gaze steady in his own, "being alone's the least of it. It's the habits of Kevin and myself I miss. The other, the being alone, one way or another, I've been alone all my life. Much as yourself, Father."

She'd barely uttered the words when the clouds parted. In the sudden spill of moonlight she looked up at the sky and said deeply, "It's come on fair."

"Aye," he answered, his voice bedded, as hers had been, in marvelment.

She tore her eyes from the sky back to him: "But I've not asked you, Father, did you have the luck fishing?"

"Oh! Enda!" he broke forth.

"So you did have the luck!" she charged. "Tell me."

"You'll not believe me."

She smiled: "You're charming me for a joke."

"A *joke*?" he asked, puffing out his chest. "Did I mention anything about a joke?"

"*Tell* me," her voice in the fur of a coax.

"I don't known how to."

"*Father—*"

He extended his arms: "Twenty-four pounds ten ounces!" he swanked.

"No!" she cried, seizing his hand. "No!"

"I'm telling you. . . . Twenty-four pounds ten ounces! It's there, back there in the boot!"

"Lord in heaven!" she trilled, "Just imagine! And everybody yammering on, complaining of how poor the season's been, *though*," her brows came together, "Catherine's niece, Bridie—it was her as married Peter Martin, they moved to Clifden, you remember?—well, Bridie's sister-in-law's nephew brought in a fourteen-pounder last week from out of one of the loughs near Kylemore. Catherine told me of it today. . . . But twenty-four pounds ten ounces!" Her eyes narrowed with glee: "Tomorrow, now, before Mass, I'll just put the word in Derrick Cavanaugh's ear. He'll spread it quick enough, and when it gets to Liam Curley—oh, he'll give with a cry they'll hear in Galway, out as he's been since the start of the season, thrashing every stretch of water in the land! Father!" she crowed, "You'll be God Himself in the pulpit tomorrow."

Witched, her eyes met his as laughter consumed them, hoot to increase, rocking her, chair-like, and bending him double over the steering-wheel. . . .

Until, after the roistering seizure, still in the bond of mirth, he looked at her, then away, then back, and in the force of a different gale told her, "You've no way of knowing how you've capped the day for me."

"Oh," she answered in her lit way, "we're that alike in our needs, Father."

Emboldened, he said, "There's no one in the world but you I wanted to see tonight."

She did not move. Her eyes remained firmly fastened in the clasp of his own. But on her face, in the moonlight, all that was earlier vivid and venturing dissolved of a sudden into a staying, balanced, and vested look which held, suspended in it and between them, all the multifarious wonders of impossibility.

He looked from her, past her, off, into the spilled shadows.

She said to him, "It's lovely for me that you came by," studying him. Then, with a tug at her shawl: "But I mustn't keep you talking all night, tomorrow being Sunday, your busy day," her eyes still on him, "though, as I'm dying to know all the details of today, could you not come on Monday at tea-time, your duties permitting of course," still watching him. "I'll have hot oatcakes," and, as he still was silent, she challenged him with: "You do like my oatcakes, do you not? You've always said you do."

"I *do*," he blurted with the sudden heart of a man who has been long at the oars and sees before him, through the mists, the post of a mooring: "You know I do."

"So we'll leave it stand for Monday."

He nodded. "Monday," he repeated. "And,"

meeting her eyes again, "you're to have a good bit of the salmon, of course."

She smiled deeply. "It'll be a ravishing treat for me."

She took a step back from the car.

He turned the ignition key. Over the engine's murr, he said: "Thank you."

"Ah," she augmented the drawing-out of the word with a skyward lift of her hand, "it's as I said, we're that alike."

"So goodnight then, Enda dear."

"You'll drive carefully, won't you."

"I will."

She livened and teased: "For the salmon's sake, of course." But her face was serious.

"I'll just watch you into the house," he said.

She crossed the yard slowly. From the door, she waved.

He called out again, "Goodnight, Enda," then turned the wheel hard to the right and started off down the track of the moonlit, homing lane.

About the Author

Jeannette Haien is well known in the United States and Europe as a concert pianist and teacher. She and her husband, a lawyer, live in Manhattan and spend a fraction of each year at their summer home in Connemara, Ireland.

Perennial Fiction Library
Harper & Row, Publishers

World-Class Writing

Title	Price	Number
_ HAWKSMOOR by Peter Ackroyd	$7.95	09-13905
_ NOVEL WITH COCAINE by M. Ageyev	$6.95	09-70004
_ TO THE LAND OF THE CATTAILS by Aharon Appelfeld	$6.95	09-71150
_ THE PROPHETEERS by Max Apple	$7.95	09-61581
_ RED SKY AT MORNING by Richard Bradford	$6.95	09-13616
_ ONE WAY OR ANOTHER by Peter Cameron	$5.95	09-14218
_ BLISS by Peter Carey	$7.95	09-13558
_ ILLYWHACKER by Peter Carey	$9.95	09-13319
_ A PERIOD OF CONFINEMENT by Moira Crone	$6.95	09-71085
_ LUISA DOMIC by George Dennison	$6.95	09-13855
_ A TALE OF PIERROT by George Dennison	$8.95	09-61698
_ THE OLD GRINGO by Carlos Fuentes	$5.95	09-70632
_ THE LOVER OF HORSES by Tess Gallagher	$6.95	09-14358
_ COLLECTED STORIES by Gabriel García Márquez	$7.95	09-13061
_ FOREVER FLOWING by Vasily Grossman	$6.95	09-13178
_ LIFE AND FATE by Vasily Grossman	$10.95	09-13848
_ YELLOWFISH by John Keeble	$7.95	09-14432
_ CONFEDERATES by Thomas Keneally	$7.95	09-14465
_ LOVE OUT OF SEASON by Ella Leffland	$7.95	09-13020
_ RUMORS OF PEACE by Ella Leffland	$7.95	09-13012
_ ORSINIAN TALES by Ursula K. Le Guin	$6.95	09-14333
_ THE WIND'S TWELVE QUARTERS by Ursula K. Le Guin	$6.95	09-14341
_ MCKAY'S BEES by Thomas McMahon	$5.95	09-13681
_ IN COUNTRY by Bobbie Ann Mason	$6.95	09-13509
_ SHILOH AND OTHER STORIES by Bobbie Ann Mason	$6.95	09-13301
_ GHOST DANCE by Carole Maso	$7.95	09-70988
_ A CANTICLE FOR LEIBOWITZ by Walter M. Miller, Jr.	$6.95	09-13210
_ MY OWN GROUND by Hugh Nissenson	$6.95	09-70756